'I'm not beaten by a few insults, Sister.' Paul's voice was dangerously quiet. 'But I am the chairman, and I don't think the committee would approve of single members acting off their own bat. In my opinion you've messed things up here. But we have two weeks. I'm sure we can sort something out.'

'If you cancel Mary's interview, I'll resign from the committee.'

'Don't be childish, Robyn. You wouldn't do that. You care too much about the hospital.'

She swung round to face him, forgetting her policy of staying apart, and avoiding the trap of those tiger-green eyes. 'I care about my sister's feelings too. Maybe caring about someone is something you wouldn't understand!'

Lancashire-born, Jenny Ashe read English at Birmingham, returning thence with a BA and RA—the latter being rheumatoid arthritis, which after barrels of various pills, and three operations, led to her becoming almost bionic, with two man-made joints. Married to a junior surgeon in Scotland, who was born in Malaysia, she returned to Liverpool with three Scottish children—now married with children of their own—when her husband went into general practice in 1966. She has written non-stop since then—articles, short stories and radio talks. Her novels just had to be set in a medical environment, which she considers compassionate, fascinating and completely rewarding.

Previous Titles

FROM SHADOW TO SUNLIGHT
CARIBBEAN TEMPTATION

TENDER MAGIC

BY

JENNY ASHE

MILLS & BOON LIMITED
ETON HOUSE   18–24 PARADISE ROAD
RICHMOND   SURREY   TW9 1SR

First published in Great Britain 1991 by Mills & Boon Limited

© Jenny Ashe 1991

Australian copyright 1991 Philippine copyright 1992 This edition 1992

ISBN 0 263 77522 4

Set in 10 on 12 pt Linotron Times 03-9201-53303 Typeset in Great Britain by Centracet, Cambridge Made and printed in Great Britain

CHAPTER ONE
April

ROBYN fastened the silver buckle round her shapely waist, not bothering to look at herself in the mirror, and smoothed back her shining hair, so different from her sister's mass of unruly curls. 'Sorry I've got to rush this morning, Mary. But the new consultant is coming and I've got to make him feel at home.'

Her sister smiled at Robyn's reflection in the mirror. It was a perfect early-April day, and the scent from the blossom outside their cottage window drifted in on the sunbeams. 'I'm sure you can do it, Bobbie.'

'Ever the optimist!' Robyn ruffled her curls. 'Ring me if you need anything.'

'Do you know what this new man is like?'

'Mr Gordon is threatening us with a fiery Welsh dragon! Howell-Jones, his name is. But he's been working in the Hammersmith in London, so he can't be all that Welsh.'

'I hope the dragon can work some Welsh magic for you.'

Robyn laughed shortly. 'Magic is the only thing that can save Chase Hey, I'm afraid. I think we have to accept the inevitable. Time is running out for the smalltown hospital. It's the greatest pity, but Barnaby has to live in the twentieth century just like any other town. See you tonight, love. Take care.'

'I'll try and work on a suitable spell!' Mary called, turning her wheelchair skilfully, and following her sister to the door. As Robyn drove off in her modest white car, she saw Mary through the driving-mirror, wheeling herself out, to enjoy the spring beauty of their small cottage garden. It would be a perfect day to do a little gardening, hoe the borders between the daffodils, and spend some time preparing the bedding plants, the seed potatoes and scarlet runners that were ready in the shed. Robyn sighed. If Chase Hey closed it would be a long drive to a Manchester or Preston hospital to find another job. She would hate to uproot Mary from the home they loved, and move to town. Yet it might become necessary.

She looked up at the second-floor window of the old grey stone hospital where she had worked since student days. Someone was waving. As Robyn parked next to a shiny red Lotus she didn't recognise, she looked up again. Sally Grey, one of her staff nurses, was mouthing something and pointing. 'He's already here!'

So the new consultant had apparently already arrived—it must be his scarlet Lotus. That was a black mark against Robyn already. It was no use telling anyone that she had to help Mary dress. She ought to have got up earlier. She ran upstairs, and hastily pinned on her cap. 'Couldn't help it. Any developments during the night I ought to be told about?'

They looked through Night Sister's notes. No dramas during the night. Thank goodness. Because any minute now the phone would summon her to the important policy meeting, and she didn't want to miss any of it. Robyn greeted her nurses, and went out to the ward to say good morning to her patients. There was a chorus of cheerful voices from those who were well enough. 'Morning', love!' 'Mornin', Sister West.'

'Lovely mornin', love!' And then came the telling phrases, showing that the patients, as well as the staff, were terribly aware of their sentence of closure. 'You're goin' to give it to 'em today, aren't you, Sister? You tell 'em what's what!' And the softer pleas from the older women, 'We'd have nowhere to go without Chase Hey. Do they know that? Our Bill couldn't manage the travellin' to visit if we was anywhere else.' 'Neither could our Jack, at his age.'

'I'll fight your corner, ladies, It's my corner too. And the good news is that we've got a new consultant today, who might be able to help.'

'Good luck, love.'

Back in her room, Sally said, 'I don't know how you manage it, having them all eating out of your hand.'

Robyn said simply, 'I love them, Sal—they're not cases, they're people.'

'I suppose having Mary has given you more practice.'

'Maybe.' Robyn got down to her paperwork, understanding Sally's complaint. Sally was a career nurse, brilliant at her books, but unable to empathise with the grumpier and more difficult patients. Robyn had hopes of Sally, but she needed a lot more patience. Then the phone rang. 'This is it, Sal!' The atmosphere was suddenly charged. She picked up the receiver.

'Could you spare an hour to meet Dr Howell-Jones and talk over our problems, Robyn?'

'You bet I can.' She crossed her fingers. Tom Gordon, the administrator, was outwardly a reserved sort of man, but he was one hundred per cent behind the campaign to save Chase Hey.

The new boy, Paul Howell-Jones, was standing beside Tom Gordon as the other staff filed in and were introduced. 'This is Robyn West, one of my nicest sisters. Robyn, Dr Paul Howell-Jones.'

She looked up into a pair of very direct green eyes in a smooth, well-shaved face topped by slightly unruly light brown hair. 'Sister West, how do you do?' A cultured voice—deep and attractively gravelly, and yes, there was a charming Welsh lilt to his words.

They shook hands—he had a firm grip. Robyn said, 'Good morning. I hope you'll like it here.'

'We have to save it first, Sister.'

'I do hope so.' And Robyn moved on as the chief consultant, John Crabtree, came dashing in, apologising for having an emergency to see to.

It was a short meeting. Eyed by the rest of the campaign committee, especially Robyn, Howell-Jones spoke briefly. 'I understand you have tried all the usual channels: patient protests, letters to MPs, that sort of thing. Now it's time for direct action, in the form of raising money for a trust fund. I know we have a year—which sounds like a long time, but isn't if we want to prove that this hospital is a viable and going concern. I propose to do a little time-and-motion to begin with. I want the reputation for efficient use of resources to go out to the world. Are you with me on that?'

They could hardly be against him. They had to try everything. But Robyn ventured to suggest, very politely, that having complete strangers watching their every move without understanding might make things more difficult. In her gentlest, most reasonable voice she said, 'Could the ward sisters do their own study, sir? It would be cheaper. I'm sure we could have the results on your desk in a couple of weeks.'

Howell-Jones fixed her with that piercing look again,

his eyes shining like a cat's across the table. 'Two weeks is half a month. Half a month is what we haven't got, Sister, because it then leaves us only eleven and a half months instead of a year.'

'It might work.'

'You should have done it earlier, then, Sister West. It's too late now for pussyfooting. However, we have twelve months. I understand there is a fund-raising event planned for each one of those months, and sometimes more than one. Well done. The sooner I meet the editor of the local paper, the better the coverage of those twelve-plus events will be. Good luck, ladies and gentlemen. It's not a small sum we have to find, and it won't be easy.'

The meeting broke up after a few more minutes. Robyn felt angry at Howell-Jones's put-down, and in her mind had already decided that, clever though he was, he was also the sort of man who never listened much to other people's opinions.

John Crabtree came to the west wing for a ward-round. He was a bluff Northerner himself, and they had been friends for years. 'By the way, Robyn, I don't know how to put this, after the way Howell-Jones spoke to you this morning. But he's taking over in my wards. I'm going to have the east wing, now that Simkins is retiring. The west wing belongs to Howell-Jones.'

'Oh, no, John!' Robyn wasn't one to moan, but she was sure that Paul Howell-Jones wouldn't make her job any easier. He was so decisive and sure of himself, so unlike gentle, approachable John Crabtree. 'Why can't Doctor Too-Big-For-His-Boots have the east wing?'

'It seems that his speciality is diabetes mellitus. He

wants somewhere where he can carry on his research. He's doing an important paper on the frequency of cardiac problems in insulin-dependent diabetics. Sorry. There's nothing I can do.'

Robyn muttered, 'Then maybe I should transfer to the east wing too. I don't like the man.'

'He did ruffle your feathers unnecessarily. Maybe that's how they get things done in London. Try not to get in his way. He might just have the guts we need to keep our campaign alive.'

'You can trust me, John. But only for the sake of the hospital.'

'Then I can bring him in this morning? I said I would have to speak to you first.'

'And I bet he told you that ward sisters should do what they're told, and don't need consulting!'

John smiled, and patted her shoulder. 'I've hardly ever seen you angry, love. But yes—he did imply there was no need. He'll need a bit of time to adjust to the fact that in Chase Hey Hospital we use good manners a lot.'

Robyn did her best to calm down, for the sake of harmony in the campaign. Chase Hey came first. It had to be saved. When the tall figure of Paul Howell-Jones loomed along the corridor and into her life she counted to ten very slowly, and gave him a smile. 'Come in, sir. Dr Crabtree is here, with the first ,atient.'

'And what is wrong with this patient?' He seemed interested only in getting on, apparently leaving all behind him breathless.

'An exacerbation of lupus. Pains in all the joints. She's settling on bed-rest and relaxation.'

'Relaxation?'

'Yes. It's a technique we've used very successfully in this ward. It takes time. . .' She paused, remembering his time-and-motion study. 'It works, sir. It's a technique they learn here, and then they can take it home with them, and use whenever they feel tense.'

'Sounds a bit cranky to me. Let's get on, then, Sister.'

They caught up with Dr Crabtree. It was fairly obvious to Robyn that the new consultant was very like Sally in his attitude to pain. He knew the correct drug treatment, but hardly ever asked the patients any questions about themselves. They were cases to be treated, not people with problems.

'Time for coffee, Robyn?' John liked his morning cup.

'The kettle is on. For you too, Dr Howell-Jones?'

'If you have the time.'

She said calmly, 'You mean if it interferes with ward duties? I don't think so, Doctor. A pause for a coffee gives us all the energy to carry on longer.' She saw John smiling behind Howell-Jones's back, and realised that he was enjoying the little verbal sparring that was going on. She turned away, and poured the boiling water over the coffee. 'I hope you don't mind instant, Dr Howell-Jones?'

'As it is purely for energy-giving purposes, Sister, I assume the taste isn't important.' He could be coolly sarcastic, all right. But Robyn forced herself to ignore his bad manners, and took the case-notes to put away, while the consultants discussed the patients with the houseman. At least Howell-Jones knew his medicine. He was familiar with all the latest research, and John enthusiastically agreed to try a couple of new drugs, which Paul said had been tested in the Hammersmith, even though the results hadn't yet been published.

Then John looked at his watch. 'Off to the east wing for me. Double duty this morning. But I'm happy to leave the ward—and Sister West—in your capable hands, Paul. You have a clinic at eleven-thirty.'

'Right.' Suddenly Robyn and Paul Howell-Jones were alone. She tried not to back away from his searching green gaze.

He said suddenly, 'You're a very pretty woman, you know.'

She looked straight at him then, taken off her guard. But, swiftly collecting herself, she replied quietly, 'Possibly. But irrelevant, surely, Doctor.'

For the first time, Howell-Jones smiled. It transformed his good looks into handsomeness, the light in his eyes becoming human, warm and a lot more approachable. 'Will you have dinner with me?'

She was taken aback by an invitation from this dragon, when so far all they had done was argue. She was also quite sure of her response. 'No, thank you.'

'Let me put it another way.' The Welsh charm was laid on. 'I'm a new boy. The best way for me to find out what makes Chase Hey tick—find its heart, if you like—is to talk to the people who are fighting to save it.'

Robyn said shortly, 'Dr Crabtree could help you there.'

'But Dr Crabtree has a wife and family. It would be presumptuous of me to expect him to give up his time with them. You, I see from your left hand, are free of family ties. It would be of great help to me, Sister West.'

She still looked him directly in the eye. Smooth, he

was—clever. Appealing to her sense of duty now. He was a master of all the tricks, she was sure. 'I'd like to help. But I'm having dinner with my sister. I couldn't let her down.'

'Bring her along.'

'No—thank you. Maybe if I stay behind after work for an hour I could answer some of your questions?'

He strolled to the window then, and looked out over the fields. 'This is nice. I don't often see cows—real Friesians. And are those horses over there for hire?'

'Yes, there's a riding stable in the dell. The farmer, Mr Bragg, has done a bit of racehorse breeding, though he has no stud at the moment.'

Howell-Jones turned from the window. Again she was almost hypnotised by his eyes as he murmured softly, 'No stud at the moment, eh? And what about you, Sister West?'

She wondered if he meant the *double entendre* with that question. To fend him off, she replied coolly, 'I really haven't time to chat, Doctor. Sorry I can't help you.'

'Maybe another night, then.' He smiled again, but less openly this time. 'Goodbye for the moment, Sister West.'

Her farewell was very curt. It wasn't in Robyn's nature to be rude, but she felt the young consultant had treated her with a great lack of sensitivity, and she wanted to be rid of him. She sat at her desk, and drew her work schedules towards her, but, though she looked at them very hard, she didn't see a word. Instead she found herself going over what green-eyed Dr Howell-Jones had said, the way he had seemed pleased at the countryside, the way he had shown an interest in Willy Bragg's horses—and the way he had sounded very sincere when he had told her she was pretty.

The hospital day was routine, with the usual streams of local visitors in the afternoon, many of whom she knew personally, and who stopped for a chat with her, with sincere expressions of gratitude for her kindness. Barnaby was a small town, and Chase Hey drew patients from a wide circle of outlying villages as well. As the day drew to a close, and the calm afternoon sun bathed the small town and its little grey hospital with warm yellow, and the nesting birds sang their bursting songs of joy in the sycamores in the hospital grounds, Robyn reflected that it took a lifetime to know and understand the heart of Chase Hey. How could she explain it to a pushy young medico with a red Lotus sports car and a brash London background? It was asking the impossible. But someone would have to try.

She had a chat with Tom Gordon before driving home. 'Don't judge him too soon, Robyn. He's a very new broom. And he asked for the job knowing about the possible closure—at interview he told them he enjoyed a challenge. I think he wants us to like him.'

'He didn't make a good start, then. Not with me.'

'To be honest, Robyn, I don't think he expected a quiet little ward sister to stand up to him as you did.'

Robyn drove home, breathing in the sweet smell of the new grass and the may blossom, out early this year with the mild spring. Meadow Cottage nestled in a cocoon of time, wreathed with age-old ivy, the pear trees in its garden planted more than a hundred years ago.

Mary was in the garden again. 'Isn't it wonderful? The sun is still warm. I've planted some nemesias and petunias along the wall, and a bed of gazanias in front of the sunflowers.'

'With a bit of help, I take it?'

'Oh, yes. Amos gave me a hand with the filling in; and he cut the grass.'

'I can smell it. It's lovely.'

'It's hotpot for dinner, so there's no peeling to be done. You can go and change, and then we'll sit out here for a while until the sun gets low. I've chilled some Mateus. You can tell me all about the meeting while we drink it.'

Robyn washed and changed into cotton trousers and a thin sweater. Mary was so uncomplaining. And so pretty, with that long fluffy light brown hair, which she looked after all by herself, in spite of her weak arms. When Robyn went down, Mary had taken herself out into the back, where Amos had flagged a sheltered area, and they could watch the sun go down between the fruit trees. Two glasses of wine were on the wooden trestle-table, sparkling pink in the late sun. Mary said, 'Well? And how was the new consultant?'

'Don't ask!'

'Oh, dear.'

Then another voice drifted across the patio from the path at the side of the house. It was a deep voice, with a gentle Welsh lilt, which Robyn had already taken a dislike to. It had disturbed her. It was a masculine voice, with a touch of gravel in it, giving its owner a hint of depravity and worldly-wisdom. 'Don't say any more, Sister—unless you want to incriminate yourself!' And Paul Howell-Jones came round the corner of the house, dressed in a casual shirt and jeans. Mary looked up with a friendly smile of approval at his very presentable appearance. Paul's face changed when he saw the wheelchair, and he paused for a moment. He came forward, however, with an outstretched hand, and a smile on his lips and in those green, green eyes. 'Good evening, Robyn's sister. It's a great pleasure to meet you. You don't look a bit alike—but I'm sure every admirer says that. I'm Paul.'

And Robyn was forced to explain. 'This is our new consultant, Mary. Paul Howell-Jones. But he *isn't* staying long.' She emphasised 'isn't'.

Mary's hand was held in Paul's strong grip for a moment. She said, 'You're very welcome, Paul. Would you care for a glass of wine?'

He turned to look at Robyn, who stood helplessly on the step. 'May I? I'd love one. It's been a long day.'

Robyn went into the little flagged kitchen, and poured a third glass. And she had thought him pushy? Pushy was too weak a word for him. What utter cheek, strolling into their little home totally uninvited. She took the glass out. Paul was already sitting beside Mary, admiring the garden, while she pointed out her particular joy, the bed of herbs, with their protective hedge of sweet lavender just beginning to bud. 'Here you are, Doctor.'

'Please call me Paul.'

'Are you on your way somewhere?' Robyn wasn't usually inhospitable. But for Paul Howell-Jones she could make an exception.

'No. I just couldn't bear to stay in the residence on such a beautiful evening. I'm exploring. I thought perhaps we could go on with our conversation that we started this morning.'

'I said I wasn't free for dinner.'

Mary said, 'Would you like to join us, Paul? There's plenty.'

He turned the green cat's eyes on Robyn. 'It would be awfully good of you. You see I'm very anxious to learn a lot more about the history of Chase Hey—the sooner the better from the point of view of the campaign to save it.' He accepted the glass of wine from her hand, and their fingers touched. He murmured, 'I think it is the Muslims who describe a paradise very like this—sun and flowers and beautiful women.' He held up his glass. 'To a long and happy friendship.'

Mary had been watching them both shrewdly. She raised her glass too. 'I'll drink to that, Paul.'

Robyn held hers, sipped but said nothing. She could have poured the wine down his confident neck! But they had been well brought up, the West sisters, and were considered gentlefolk. So Robyn sipped her wine too, and eventually took a seat, at Paul's insistence, at the trestle-table beside him.

'You wanted to tell me about the heart of Chase Hey, Robyn,'

Robyn said quietly, 'It lies in respect for tradition, love of the countryside, and thoughtfulness of people to people, Paul. It is gentleness and helpfulness. It is staunch loyalty to what we have learned over the centuries to be right values. It is not being ashamed of being thought old-fashioned, not rushing and pushing to be trendy and modern just for the sake of it.'

Paul's eyes were hooded. 'You put it very well, Robyn. The sad thing is that these values and the new government economy-drive don't mix.'

'So we might as well give up on Chase Hey now, you mean?'

The budding lavender scent was strong, as the sun dipped behind the hills, and a slight breeze rustled the branches of the pear trees, white with blossom, but still bare of leaves. He said, 'I don't give up easily. I've been thinking of this trust fund. If we can show that we can raise the necessary cash ourselves. . .What do you two think?'

And Mary said, her blue eyes shining with enthusiasm and hope, 'You can do it. I know you can. If everyone works together.' And she looked first at Paul, and then at Robyn. 'If we can't find an accountant, or a financial adviser, who's willing to help the hospital that has been part of everyone's birth and death since Victoria ruled this land, then Chase Hey isn't what I thought it was.' She paused, and looked again from Paul to Robyn with bright, hopeful eyes. 'I don't make promises easily. But I know we have what it takes to fight for what we think is right.'

'Bravo, Mary. I agree.'

'Thank you, Paul. What do you say, Bobbie?'

Paul's enthusiasm seemed honest. Robyn would have looked at him directly—except for the fact that his green eyes had a disturbing effect on her heartbeat. And he had proved himself to be insolent. Even John Crabtree had noticed it. Paul Howell-Jones was an outsider. He wanted success only for his own glory. Chase Hey meant nothing to him. Yet somehow, with Mary's blue eyes and Paul's green ones directed at her, Robyn couldn't put her objections into words. 'What can I say but—here's to Chase Hey?'

CHAPTER TWO
April—May

PAUL HOWELL-JONES had been busy settling into his new routine, and his new quarters in the hospital residence wing, and Robyn West was relieved, because he had less time to annoy her. She had to admit that his conversation at dinner had been politely restrained, that he had listened a lot to what the sisters had to say about Barnaby, and said very little about himself. On reflection, even this was slightly unsettling.

It was some time later when she drove home one day, and Mary met her at the door of the cottage with a beaming smile. Hair framed her sister's face and curled on her shoulders, and Robyn looked sadly at her, knowing how beautiful she was, and what a wonderful wife she would make for some lucky man, if only she could get out more and meet the right people. Mary had always been the pretty one at school, the extrovert, while Robyn's quiet manner, smooth complexion and straight hair didn't make the same impact. Yet it had had to be Mary who caught polio.

No more dancing lessons. Robyn refused to go without Mary. No more riding at Willy Bragg's stables, and no more boyfriends. Yet Mary West had never once complained. And today she was excited. 'Bobbie, guess who's been to see us? The editor of the *Barnaby Recorder*! He heard about my herbs, and wants to do an article.'

19

'That's great, Mary. Who told him?'

'Jackie.' Jackie was the owner of the health shop, who bought herbs from Mary, and had them processed by a pharmacist in Accrington. 'But Bobbie, wait till I tell you my idea! Jackie wants to expand her business. You have space in the hospital. You told me there was room going to waste. Why don't you arrange for Chase Hey to have its own little shopping arcade? Jackie would love the extra space. Charge her rent and put it to the action fund!'

Robyn dumped her handbag and the groceries on the floor, and ran to the bureau. 'Mary, you're a genius. Come over here, and let's try to get this on paper for the committee. Jackie wants a herbalist's premises. I'm absolutely certain I could persuade Jo at the village flower shop that an outlet on hospital premises would be a winner. And refreshments—the Friends of Chase Hey don't make much with their little coffee-bar. We could get someone to do real coffee, and home-made scones. Fresh fruit juices. And jam! How about Jilly Forshaw's jam? God knows we have enough good cooks in our road alone.'

Mary had wheeled herself to Robyn's shoulder, where she watched, her hair hanging over her face, as her sister scribbled their ideas down. 'I thought we could get the editor—his name's Ross Cartwright, by the way, and he went to our school—to combine the article on herbs with a bit of publicity for the hospital. What do you think? Could you get things moving? I remember Paul saying that you need the Press on your side.'

'It sounds fantastic. All the lucky firms involved would get a bit of free advertising.' She paused. 'Of course, there would need to be a bit of clearing up—

and rebuilding. That's going to cost money we don't have. And I'm not sure how the law stands on planning permission.'

Mary smiled, unwilling to allow her enthusiasm to be dampened. 'But get enough people interested, and the impetus is already there. Let's do it, Bobbie. Ring your Dr Paul right now!'

Robyn sat back and laughed. 'Mary, do you mind if I get out of this uniform and into a hot bath? It's a brilliant idea, but we do have twelve months! And guess who's been admitted today—again?'

'Don't tell me! Philomena Gorsey! What is it this time? I thought you got her off sniffing glue.'

'Oh, yes, poor soul. It isn't that.' Robyn sat on the arm of the sofa, her eyes thoughtful. 'She's just— inadequate, I'm afraid. Sad little thing. Not even mentally ill. The infirmary just hasn't the time to deal with people like her. But her GP has asked us to have her for a week or so. She's hurt her arm in some way, and John Crabtree thinks it was self-inflicted, to get her more sympathy.'

'I'm sorry for her. But don't you see? It's for people like Philomena that we simply must stay open. We're her lifeline. Without Chase Hey, what would her GP do?' Mary turned to the kitchen. 'It's made me even more determined to fight, Sis. You go and change. I'll put the potatoes on.'

'And I'll promise to see Paul straight after his ward-round.'

'Tomorrow? Not tonight?'

'Tomorrow. I have to work with him, remember? He's a bit like a dynamo on two legs—always three steps ahead of anyone else. Don't worry, Mary—once he takes to the idea, he'll have Barnaby spinning!'

The scent of the fresh new lavender sprigs was strong when Robyn came back to the sitting-room. Mary was filling a large square basket with the fragrant leaf sprays, and covering them with foil to keep in the goodness. 'Jackie wants to pick up some supplies on her way to work in the morning.'

'I don't know what she would do without you and your garden.'

Mary looked pleased. 'Wait till the flowers come. And there'll be even bigger orders if she gets a second shop in Chase Hey.'

Next day Robyn spent a long part of her morning talking to little Philomena Gorsey. 'How is your boy-friend, Phil?'

'If you mean Kevin Bleeding Halfpenny, he's gone off to Salford to work, and never told me he was going.' Philomena was one of life's victims—thin and pale, with a trusting, simple attitude to life that was constantly causing her pain. Robyn dressed the wound in her upper arm herself, wrapping the bandages carefully, and noticing as she worked that Philomena didn't seem to mind the pain. It was indeed probably attention she wanted.

'And you still like him, Phil?' she asked gently.

Philomena looked at her as though half scared to speak. Her voice was a whisper. 'I think I'm pregnant, Sister.'

Robyn hid her sudden intake of breath. With professional cool she didn't really feel, she said, 'Then I'll get one of the midwives to come and see you later, dear. Don't worry. We'll sort you out.'

The expression on the thin face was one of total relief. Robyn sighed again, as later, after ringing Obstetrics about their possible new client, she took the plan of action she had worked out with Mary, and at coffee-time laid it before Paul Howell-Jones. 'My sister grows excellent herbs. Top quality.'

'And I was very pleased to be shown round her garden. She's very knowledgeable. Your dinner was proof of that.'

'Not just for cooking. She sells them to a herbalist.'

Paul's tone changed. 'Oh, one of those.'

'You may not think much of village remedies, but ——'

'Alternative medicine is. . .not entirely a load of rubbish—but not applicable to real disease. We're in the realm of micro-pharmacology now. Gene biology. Herbs are for simple minds. Plants were all very well before real pharmacology was developed. All right for witches and wise women—sometimes they used the right remedies out of sheer luck—but totally out of date now.'

Robyn's voice was tart. 'Are you calling Mary a witch?'

'No, of course not. But you have to know what I mean.'

Robyn said coldly, 'I was going to tell you that the editor of the *Recorder* is planning an article, with photographs, on Mary and Jackie. Last night we worked out a really exciting plan to combine the article with publicity for the hospital. You see—this is what we thought. . .' and she placed the paper before Paul. 'If we could get this idea off the ground before the "May Day at Chase Hey" fête it would get a lot more people interested in our campaign, and more people coming to the fête.'

Paul held the paper in one hand, and looked at it carefully, the green eyes unreadable. He said, 'You do realise that this a hospital? Having herbalists on the premises seems a crazy idea—it's as though we endorse their tomfool ideas.'

'We don't have to endorse them. We charge them rent towards the action fund. That's hard-headed business, Paul, not coven economics!'

'What other tenants have you thought of? Acupuncturists? Naturopathy? Chiropractice? Maybe voodoo? Are you trying to close the hospital even before the year is up?'

Infuriated by his dismissive sarcasm, Robyn said, 'You're over-reacting, Paul. This is planning! Sensible use of facilities! I thought we could have a flower shop, and maybe a small whole-food snack bar. You can't possibly turn your high-tech nose up at that.' She turned away, and banged some folders away, wondering why she had ever admired this man's dynamism. He was blind to a perfectly good money-making opportunity. 'Don't you want to save the hospital?'

'Not by herbalism, thank you. It's counter-productive. Can't you see the headlines—"Hospital Runs on Superstition"? It won't work, Robyn.'

She turned back angrily to face him. 'Well, you'll have to tell Ross Cartwright yourself, then. Mary's already asked him to interview her at the fête on May the first. You do know it's in the hospital grounds?'

'Oh, God. Robyn, I like your sister very much, and I think you're the prettiest creature in Barnaby. But I wish you'd waited to discuss this properly before you jumped in at the deep end. Don't you see, it will do more harm than good?'

'We had no time. There's only a fortnight to the fête. And we know Barnaby—it will do more good than harm!'

He threw her carefully written plan on the desk, reached out and caught her hand. Drawing her towards him, Paul said, 'Maybe you'd like to see my ideas too? I don't want to offend you, Robyn, but I thought I was the chairman of the action committee, not you and Sister Mary. Look here.' He undid his white coat, and took a folded paper from his inner pocket.

Robyn felt the warmth of his body, and took in the quality of his fine lawn shirt, the Harrods label on his tie. 'At the fête I was going to make a speech of welcome. I hope there will be several prominent and wealthy citizens there—they've been invited, especially the district health authority lot, and their chairman, Swainson Black. Then I shall ask them all to consider making a covenant in favour of Chase Hey. It will be a sort of group pressure—if one does it, others will be too ashamed to appear mean, so they'll all do it.' He squeezed her hand, and for a moment there was a hint of a smile in the green eyes, and Robyn had to stop herself gazing at its magic, which already, she realised, had the potential to affect her strength of will. 'Believe me, I'm a dab hand at that kind of speech. I know what I'm doing. Now if your Mr Cartwright comes gallumphing in with his photographers and reporters, wanting to take pictures of little old ladies in flowery hats who make camomile tea and jasmine soup, our backers won't want to put good money into an anachronism, will they? Herbs went out with the witches, and are perpetuated by the cranks; and we don't want them back. What sort of go-ahead, high-tech hospital will Chase Hey look like? You tell me, Robyn.'

Robyn said very quietly, 'And what does poor Philomena want with high-tech? It's caring nursing she needs. That doesn't change with every new scientific invention! So will you please let me go?' She tried to withdraw her hand from his, but he held it tighter, so she stared at him levelly, and said, 'If I were a businessman I'd think Chase Hey was being forward-looking and sensible, maximising its assets.'

'Sensible?' Paul laughed then. 'Sensible!'

Robyn's voice was cold. 'I would have thought that by using all the vacant property on the grounds, and making the tenants pay rent towards the upkeep of the hospital, we would prove that we were business-minded, and determined to keep Chase Hey going, whatever cuts the government and the district health authority have to make.'

Paul, still holding her hand, rose slowly from his chair, and put his other arm around her, pulling her very close against his starched white coat, so that she smelt its cleanness, and, under it, the warmth and maleness she had already been affected by. Speaking with his lips very close against her cap, he murmured, 'You really are the loveliest creature—especially when you're angry. Do you know how your eyes flash?'

Robyn tried to break free, but his strength was greater than hers, and she was forced to stand within the circle of his arm. She didn't look into his face as she said, trying to keep her voice steady, 'It isn't a very clever ruse, you know—using sexism when you've been beaten in an argument. In fact, it's rather pitiful.'

He let her go then, and she took two steps away from him to the window of her office. His voice was dangerously quiet. 'I'm not beaten by a few insults, Sister. But I am the chairman, and I don't think the committee would approve of single members acting off their own bat. In my opinion you've messed things up here. But we have two weeks. I'm sure we can sort something out.'

'If you cancel Mary's interview, I'll resign from the committee.'

'Don't be childish, Robyn. You wouldn't do that. You care too much about the hospital.'

She swung round to face him, forgetting her policy of staying apart, and avoiding the trap of those tiger-green eyes. 'I care about my sister's feelings too. Maybe caring about someone is something you wouldn't understand!'

Paul was silent for a moment. Then he turned towards the door. 'I have a clinic in five minutes. And I want to spare young Philomena a few moments. I won't cancel anything this time, Robyn. But will you meet me halfway, and keep the photographer in a corner of the field, away from me? Just you and your sweet sister and your little old ladies?'

'All right. But I'd like it discussed in committee. I have that right.'

'Very well.' Paul opened the door. Then he turned and looked at her very directly. 'You make a powerful antagonist, Robyn. I wonder if you would be as passionate as a friend?' He was outside and along the corridor before Robyn recovered from the force of those words.

On the day of the fête, Robyn dressed carefully. She wasn't one of the organisers—that was for the Friends of Chase Hey, who had time on their hands. Robyn had Mary to see to, and never volunteered for anything in her spare time. But she decided it was important for the action committee to look capable, and she discarded a pretty full-skirted dress that she would normally have worn in favour of a trim little suit.

Mary came out of the bedroom. 'How do I look?'

'Lovely. Just lovely.' Mary was wearing a white Victorian lace blouse, with a cameo at her neck. Her hair fell shining on her shoulders, and over her calipers she wore black velvet trousers. Robyn said, 'I hope Jackie doesn't let you down by being too overdressed.'

'How could she? You know how fashion-conscious she is.'

'Fashion-conscious? Over-the-top mostly!' It wouldn't have mattered—Jackie's eccentricity of dress was part of her charm. Yet would it have the same effect on fussy Paul Howell-Jones? Robyn was neat and proper in her cream linen suit over a black low-necked blouse, with the jade pendant their missionary father had given her lending a touch of warm oriental green. She helped Mary into the car, and folded the chair into the back. 'Thank goodness for the sun. I love May Day, don't you?'

'So much—it's so timeless. The games, and the flowers, and the parade! And especially the kids round the maypole.'

Robyn's eyes clouded, as she remembered again how Mary had used to love to dance. But she said, trying to be light-hearted, 'I shall enjoy every minute, as long as Paul Howell-Jones stays at the other side of the field.' She started the engine, and they set off along the familiar country road.

Mary said, 'I know you and he started off on the wrong foot. But he isn't all bad, you know, Bobbie. I really like him.'

Robyn said guardedly, 'He's a good doctor. But I don't like men with closed minds.' She giggled suddenly. 'I do want to be there when he sees Jackie for the first time. He thinks she's a little old lady!'

The grey stone hospital was set in rolling green fields, with centuries-old oak trees shading the pathways, luxuriant sycamores, and a sea of bluebells underneath them. Stalls were set up at one side, and the little Brownies who were to dance round the maypole were being rounded up, in their gathered skirts and white mob-caps, to go round the wards, to visit those patients who were too sick to come down and watch the fun.

'Hi there, comrades!' Jackie Darcy was a tall, confident woman of about thirty-five, whose county voice and accent were at variance with her wild and original style of dress. Jackie favoured long full skirts, cloaks and high-heeled boots. Today she wore a slim-fitted black dress and black boots, with a blaze of scarlet in the form of a Paisley shawl around one shoulder. Anyone less like a little old lady would be hard to imagine. 'Who do I speak to about the rent for the new shop? By the way, I've found you another tenant, a real artist. How many spaces have you got?'

'I'll take you round later. It used to be the old outpatients' building, before they built the new annexe. The architect says that he can make about eight units round the outside, and suggests a few tables round a paved floor in the middle for coffees.'

'A sort of arcade? Sounds super. My friend Nigel is having a bit of success with his water-colours. Maybe we could use the wall space as a gallery? It would bring people in—after all, that's what you want, isn't it?'

Robyn said, 'It sounds fantastic, Jackie. But I have this reactionary chairman who likes to veto everything I suggest. I'll introduce you later. Right now I can see Ross Cartwright on his way, in his favourite old Aran sweater. Never was one to dress up, was Ross. I remember him vaguely at our old school, a few years ahead of me. Let's get you and Mary in a corner with him. Which stall is yours?' The local newspaper editor was youngish and shambling, with a baggy sweater, a warm grin and a mop of untidy brown hair. Jackie led them to her stall, where culinary herbs and spices were interspersed with cures for rheumatism, piles and backache. Robyn hoped Paul didn't come around prying, as Ross made copious notes in shorthand, and the photographer took a series of shots of Jackie and Mary. Robyn left them to it. She thought she had better patrol the area, to keep Paul Howell-Jones away from Jackie's wares.

But Paul found Robyn first. 'Hello, Bobbie.'

She swung round, recognising that deep attractive voice at once, and hoping he didn't notice her spontaneous smile of welcome. 'Paul!' Somehow she didn't even mind his using the pet name that only Mary was allowed to use.

He looked elegant, in a country tweed suit and shining brogues, his light brown hair waving back from a square forehead. She realised suddenly that he wasn't alone. 'I'd like to introduce you to Victoria Alexander, a friend from London.' And he put a cherishing hand on the arm of the blonde beauty beside him, who was dressed in a clinging wool dress of dark green, which showed off a superb model's figure and long slim legs.

'How do you do?' Robyn shook hands. A very close friend, obviously. And one couldn't blame him. She had a flawless skin, beautifully made-up large blue eyes, and fashionably careless blonde curls, falling casually on slim padded shoulders. Robyn noticed that even John Crabtree was eyeing the lovely Victoria behind his wife's back.

Paul said, 'Robyn is one of our staunchest fighters, Vicki. Robyn, don't go away. I want to introduce you to the health authority chairman. He's a hard-headed businessman, so you have your chance to put him in his place.'

'I take it you're joking.'

'Only a little. I expect you to call a spade a spade. I think Swainson Black is the type of man who appreciates straight talking.'

Robyn turned to Victoria. 'I'm sure he must have told you I'm the local bully. I really don't know where he got that idea from.' And she smiled as innocently as she could, aware that her slight appearance and quiet voice made it hard to believe she could bully anyone.

Victoria's voice was aristocratic and slightly bored. 'I know he can be a frightful tease, my dear. But what worries me is those big brown eyes of yours. Paul can be very susceptible, you know.'

Robyn laughed, embarrassed, remembering being embraced very close against that elegant manly chest only a couple of weeks or so ago, and told that she was very lovely. 'No need to worry. Nurses know doctors far too well ever to fall for one.'

'Not what I've heard, Robyn.' Victoria looked around as the accordion music began for the maypole dance. 'I say, who is that striking woman in red?'

Robyn saw Paul look over with interest, and his eyebrows raise as he saw Jackie. Exultingly innocent, Robyn said, 'Oh, that's the little old lady who runs the herbalist's stall. I expect she tells fortunes as well, and could probably run you up a little spell if you crossed her palm with silver!'

Victoria failed to notice the irony in Robyn's voice. 'I say, how absolutely marvellous. A real Romany, is she?'

Paul, however, knew Robyn better, and while Victoria's attention was taken he bent and whispered in Robyn's ear, 'I'll get you later, Sister West!'

Robyn excused herself quickly. 'I must find Mary. The dancing will soon be starting.'

After the simple, traditional maypole dancing, which was charming and timeless, and brought back Robyn's days as a Brownie, and left tears in Mary's eyes, Paul Howell-Jones found a space and a microphone. He was right. His speech made everyone laugh, but at the same time reminded them all of the seriousness of the imminent closure of Chase Hey.

'Ladies and gentlemen, three hundred and fifty thousand pounds is what we need to set up a trust fund. There are valid reasons why this money could arguably be better spent at one of the larger district hospitals. But we in Barnaby know what would be lost forever if Chase Hey closes, and we aren't going to let it happen!' There were cheers and whistles. If goodwill could have saved the hospital it was already saved. But hard economic facts were all that mattered now, and Robyn was annoyed that Paul hadn't already taken up her ideas with the committee. Today had been a perfect opportunity to promote their new arcade.

'Miss West?'

She turned to see Ross Cartwright at her elbow. 'Hello Mr Cartwright. You've finished your interviews?'

'I've got some great shots, and your sister's life

story.' He stopped, and Robyn could see from his face that he was moved. He went on, 'I remember the West sisters at school. I'm very sorry that Mary. . .' He paused. 'She tells me you won't mind my calling at the house to take shots of the cottage and the garden.'

'Of course not.'

There was another pause in the conversation. 'You look sad, Sister West.'

She smiled then, appreciating his perception. Ross Cartwright was clearly not as absent-minded as he looked. 'I had hoped you would do some sort of coverage for Chase Hey,' she admitted.'In spite of all the merry-making, it feels a bit like a wake. Internal wrangling, and all that, yet we all want the same thing.'

'May I talk to you about that? I gather something is going on. Mary told me. I'd like to help. I've already got the *Recorder*'s photographer going round doing group snaps for your cause.'

He seemed sincere. Robyn said, 'That's absolutely wonderful. I had the impression you thought we were a lost cause. Through your paper we could reach most of the population—and we have to depend on the people of Barnaby, because who else will back us?'

Ross eyed her carefully. 'Maybe we could have a meal and talk this over?'

'I'd appreciate it. Are you thinking of one article, or a series?'

Ross smiled, and she knew from the look in his eyes that Mary had won him over completely. 'Robyn I'd like to adopt your cause. Stick with it until we win. It wouldn't do the *Recorder* any harm, either, to be seen to want to help the town.'

'Mr Cartwright——'

'Make it Ross, please?'

'I don't know how to thank you.'

Then, suddenly, Paul was there with them. 'Excuse me, but aren't you the editor of the *Recorder*? I'm Paul Howell-Jones, chairman of the action committee. I've been wanting a chat with you. Got some ideas you might be able to use.' He held out his hand.

Ross looked at him with a certain air of resentment. He took the proffered hand briefly and reluctantly. It was clear to Robyn that Ross didn't like Paul's dynamic and dominating approach, and preferred to make his decisions slowly and without pressure. Ross said coolly, 'Maybe, Doctor. Call my secretary for an appointment. I'll think it over. Bye, Robyn.'

Robyn watched Cartwright as he turned proudly, and walked away. Well done, she thought. Even though Ross had already committed himself to the Cause, he was making it very clear to Paul that he wasn't a man to be pushed around. Just what Paul Howell-Jones needed!

CHAPTER THREE
June

COUNCILLOR CHRISTOPHER SWAINSON BLACK had been a prominent citizen all his life, crowning his illustrious career as a top solicitor by becoming chairman of the Barnaby and district health authority. In his black tie and dinner-jacket over a portly frame, he looked every inch the typical country alderman.

Robyn had been seated next to him in the Chase Hey best dining-room. 'You don't have to tell me your sob-stories, Sister West. I've heard nothing else for the past six months, and I sympathise most strongly. But you know as well as I do that you can't run a hospital on sympathy, and the money would be better spent going towards the new MR scanner at the infirmary. You know that, in your heart, don't you?'

The action committee were having a small formal dinner together, several weeks after the fête, and had invited Mr Black to join them, as Paul said, to make sure he was kept fully informed of their plans and progress, but also, as everyone knew but didn't say, to have the chance of playing on his sympathy. Caterers, i.e., Jilly Forshaw and her cousin Phoebe, had been called in, to save staff overtime.

Paul had placed Robyn next to the councillor, with express instructions to charm him with her wit, and touch his heart with her sincerity. It wasn't working. She replied to his question. 'I know technology is important, obviously, Mr Black, but I've found that we often get excellent lasting cures by nothing more than personal nursing and real caring.'

'That, Sister, is twaddle, in this day and age.'

Robyn said, fuming inwardly, 'If you say so. But I could take you round my ward right now, and you could ask the patients themselves. They don't ask for much, sir. Only to be looked after while they are ill.'

'I don't mean to be rude, my dear, but the doctors are there to find out what's wrong with you and to cure it. For the first they need up-to-date diagnostic aids, and for the second they need drugs and surgery.'

Robyn smiled rather sadly. 'It's clear you're a healthy man, Mr Black. You've never been in hospital. You've never needed to be cared for.'

'True. I've lived well. But I gave up cigars three years ago, and took up a daily walk. That's enough alternative medicine for me. People should take control of their own lives by healthy eating and a sober life.'

It seemed time for Robyn to give up too, and she talked about other things. 'The garden party should bring in a tidy sum.'

Later, as the guests mingled and chatted in the late sun, on the patch of lawn outside the administration block, Robyn was cornered by Paul. 'Any luck?'

'No. He's as blind as you are in some respects.'

'And what does that mean?' His voice was grim and hurt, but Robyn was no longer impressed by someone who professed to care for their hospital, but didn't want to listen to her kind of reason. 'I'm working my guts out for you and your little hospital, and you call me blind.'

'Where tenderness and the personal touch are con-

cerned, Paul, you think like Black, and like Sally—
that they don't matter.'

'You mean I have little faith in that mumbo-jumbo
with herbs and homeopathic micro-dosage?'

'I mean methods that work, and I know I'm right.'

He said, 'Have it your way, Robyn. I hate quarrel-
ling with you, you know, except that it makes your
eyes look quite magnificent.' Robyn turned away,
angry and blushing at the cheek of the man. He went
on, 'By the way, your newspaper man seems a bit of a
mangel-wurzel.'

Robyn smiled at Paul's obvious pique. She had seen,
and was pleased by the way Ross Cartwright had
totally ignored Paul when he'd tried to bully his own
ideas into the newspaper coverage of the hospital
campaign. 'I don't think you went about things in quite
the most tactful way. But don't worry. I had a chat
with him later, and he's willing to do a regular "hospital spot" for us.'

Paul looked uncomfortable. 'Thanks. I didn't mean
to sound rude, you know.'

'I know that, because I know you by now, Paul, and
I think—only think, mind you—that your heart's in
the right place.'

His ruffled feathers smoothed, Paul appeared flat-
tered. 'May I walk you home? It's a beautiful evening,
and we could both do with a gentle stroll to get Mr
Swainson Black out of our hair.'

'But it's out of your way.'

'Don't make difficulties, Bobbie.'

She felt herself blush, as he again used the name
only Mary usually was allowed to use. It sounded very
sweet and intimate in Paul's deep gravelly voice, and
she rather hoped he would say it again, as they said

goodnight to the others, and walked towards the hospital gates.

'You look after Mary very well.'

Robyn said quickly, 'It isn't that she asks me to, you know. We're just good friends as well as sisters. But we don't interfere in each other's life.'

'Isn't there a song about you two? Something about sisters—devoted sisters—and men coming between them?' He was teasing her now, and she was happy enough to laugh with him. Then he said, suddenly serious, 'Why aren't you married?'

Robyn looked up at his handsome profile, and he turned and met her look. She said, 'It isn't because of Mary, if that's what you mean.'

'So why is it?'

'Simple. Because—I haven't fallen in love with anyone.' And she felt her cheeks grow warm again at his keen green-eyed gaze. 'Isn't that a good enough reason?'

Paul nodded. They were drawing near to the cottage, and the moon was glowing white through delicate new leaves in the hedgerow, the smell of honeysuckle heavily sweet on the evening air. He stopped walking, and they stood close together in the velvet night. 'You look especially beautiful in moonlight, Bobbie. I wish I could see you like this more often. We seem always to be arguing, don't we? And it's such a waste of time.' She knew he would kiss her, and, though she didn't think it a very good idea, she found herself powerless, because of her own need, to evade his enfolding arms. In fact, somehow by his words, his gentleness and the caressing depth of his voice, he had roused in her a mood of languid sensuality, in the sweet setting of calm beauty that surrounded them. For a moment she responded to his lips, and felt his arms tighten around her as he kissed her again more boldly and ardently, his lips forceful and hungry.

She realised then that she had indeed missed out on this side of life. Since a schoolboy crush had gone away to university and never returned to Barnaby Robyn had busied herself with passing her exams, and making a full and satisfying life out of her nursing. In the arms of Paul Howell-Jones new ideas and instincts began to wake and unfold like tendrils from a sleeping plant, filling her body with excitement and longing. Scared suddenly, she took her arms from his firm torso, and pushed them against his chest. 'That's enough.'

He moved backwards, but kept hold of her shoulders. His voice was very husky as he said, 'Are you sure, Sister West? Do you really want to be left alone? It seems to me that you spend too much time alone with your sister, and not enough learning to live life.'

Fighting the urge to sink back into his embrace, Robyn said, 'I think that's my own decision, and none of your business.' He took his hands away very slowly, letting them slide down her arms before taking them away altogether. The sensation this roused in her was suddenly strong, and made her voice sharp with anxiety at her own bodily reactions. 'I must go in.'

He leaned against the gatepost, looking at her as though he didn't want to look away. 'It's June already, my little friend. Spring is almost over, and, before you know it, it will be too late. I'm talking about you, Bobbie, not the seasons of the year.'

The tension between them was almost unbearable. Robyn could think of no reply. In the back garden of the cottage, a nightingale trilled its liquid notes, and

Robyn knew she had to get away from the web of
magic this experienced man was weaving so successfully and so cleverly. Feeling vulnerable and very
naïve, she managed to croak a feeble 'Goodnight,'
before turning and almost running into the path and
up to the back door.

She lay awake for a long time, her blood racing and
her body alive and alert. How would she face him next
morning at work, knowing that he had proved what
physical control he had over her? If only he were
someone else—someone more suitable for her, instead
of a high-powered London consultant who was only in
Barnaby to do a job, and with whom she had so very
little in common. It would be crazy to allow herself to
fall for him. Robyn tossed and turned, and even began
to hope, in the feverishness of her imagination, that
Chase Hey would close, as the only way she could
imagine being able to get away from Paul Howell-
Jones.

Mary made things worse. 'When are you going to
invite Paul to dinner again? He's been to the shop
several times, Bobbie—I do believe he's beginning to
take an interest in what we do. He borrowed a book
from Jackie—*The Natural Way*. Said he wanted to find
out what all the fuss is about.'

'He did what?' Robyn's voice rose an octave.

'Borrowed a book on natural remedies.'

'The smooth operator! Don't trust him, Mary. He's
only doing it for effect.'

'I still think you ought to invite him round. You do
like him, don't you, Bobbie?'

Like him? She liked him too much in spite of hating
his outlook. She liked his sense of humour, and the
way he treated little Philomena with genuine respect

for her feelings, even though medically he was more concerned about her injured arm than about her wounded feelings because her Kevin had walked out on her. Even when they argued, Robyn would watch Paul's eyes, keen and intelligent as he put his point of view in that lilting deep Welsh voice, and recall some of the sweet words he had spoken to her in the moonlight. 'I'll ask him round if there's a good reason, not just out of the blue.'

Mary hesitated, and Robyn could see her trying to find the right words. 'Well, you see, I've asked Ross to come to dinner at the end of the month, and I thought—I mean, if you don't mind—it would make the table even if we asked Paul as well.'

Robyn looked carefully at Mary for some sign of why she invited Ross. 'I didn't realise you were on visiting terms.'

'It's—about the hospital campaign really. He asked when it would be convenient to talk to us both about who to write about next. He's done that piece on the May Day thing, and that super article on John Crabtree. He say's he's looking for a different angle.'

Robyn nodded. 'He did mention something about a meal together last time we met. OK, then, I'll ask Paul. But they didn't get on very well at first. Ross was definitely not interested in being taught his job by a trumped-up London consultant.'

'That's another reason! We could get them to bury the hatchet at the same time. They ought to be working together!'

'And Ross wants a new angle, eh?' Robyn was beginning to see the possibilities in Ross's articles. 'I think I'll have an angle for him. I think little Philomena's having nowhere else to go would make quite a point. OK,

Mary, I'll definitely invite Paul as well. It could be quite a party!'

She greeted Paul in the ward next morning quite casually, reserving her invitation until they were alone. But Robyn was kept busy, and there seemed no chance of being alone in her room when Paul was there. Sally was complaining about the patients. 'Mrs Wood is a real pest, Robyn. I can't see how you have the patience with her.'

'Because I know why she's a pest, that's how. You can't be a successful nurse unless you have sympathy with people, Sal, see things from her side. She's a widow, and her daughter won't have her to stay, because the daughter's husband doesn't want her living with them in case it becomes a habit.'

'They'd have her to stay if she didn't grumble about everything so much.'

Robyn smiled. 'The real reason you don't like her is because you think she's malingering, isn't it, Sally? You only like to look after genuine illness. You don't have any sympathy for those whose symptoms are psychosomatic?'

'I suppose you're right.'

'But the symptoms are real enough to her.'

'She's taking a bed that someone else could use.'

Robyn was patient. 'Put the kettle on, Sal. Now listen to me, while I explain. If we give Mrs Wood time and understanding now there's a chance she'll come to terms with an awkward son-in-law, and find other interests. If we throw her out because she isn't physically ill she'll be back here with yet more symptoms. I want to help her understand why she gets all these aches and pains—that's the only way to cure them.'

'You mean you want to spend a lot of valuable time just talking, don't you? Just the way you sit by that little pregnant idiot and try to make her see reason. She'll stay here forever as long as you do that!'

'No Sal, not this time. I'm not going to sit and talk to Mrs Wood or to Philomena Gorsey. I want you to do it.'

'Me? But I'm the last person——'

'That's why you're going to do it.'

'I wouldn't know where to begin.' Sally was reluctant. 'I'll fail, Robyn—you know I will. And what do I say to Philomena? Grow some brains?'

Paul Howell-Jones came in then. 'Has the houseman done the ward-round?'

'Yes, Doctor. I'll call him for you.' Robyn remembered something then, and added, 'By the way, Doctor—Sally is having a bit of trouble with Mrs Wood. Do you by any chance have that book on nature's way? I think it might help Sal to treat the patient.'

Sally stared. 'You read books like that, Doctor?'

Paul looked at Robyn with a wry grin, fully aware that she had mentioned the book on purpose to tease him. 'I picked it up out of curiosity, Sally. You can have it—I haven't opened it yet. Let Jackie have it back, won't you? What are Mrs Wood's symptoms again, Robyn?'

'Palpitations, Doctor, with no organic cause found. Depression and anxiety state, and insomnia.'

'And a nasty habit of grumbling about them all the time,' Sally added.

Paul said, 'Now wait a minute, Sally. That sounds ever so slightly intolerant. Is that a kettle boiling?' Robyn made coffee for the three of them, and Paul went on with his mug in his hand, 'I suppose I prescribed sleeping tablets for her?'

'Yes. And anti-depressants.'

Paul nodded. 'Right. Well, for a start, I want her up and about. Lying in bed moaning won't cure her. 'Sally—go and do her temp and BP, and then tell her I believe she's getting better and won't need the tablets soon.'

'That's cheating, Doctor.'

'Not really. It's Robyn's black magic. When the illness is in the mind, then the cure is in the mind, right, Robyn?'

'You have been reading the book!'

'Not much.' But he avoided her gaze. 'But I do understand psychological medicine. The only trouble is that it's time-consuming. You have to have time to listen. Think you could try it, Sally?'

'I'll have a go.'

'And explain that the pills work best after a two-mile walk.'

'You don't mean it!'

'It's true. Excercise and a good diet will do more for her than anything else.' Sally went off down the ward with her sphyg, and Paul turned to Robyn with a wink. 'Mumbo-jumbo. But I'm prepared to admit that there may be some common sense in some of it. This type of patient needs someone to care. Her life is empty. Once Mrs Wood believes we've given her something personally prescibed for her, I can back her up by occasional out-patient encouragement. Another satisfied customer.'

'What prescription did you have in mind?'

'Patchouli. It contains a natural anti-depressive.

Some of these old remedies are based on sound pharmacological sense.'

Robyn couldn't help herself bursting out laughing. 'You *have* been reading the book!' she said again.

'It's limited in its scope, but for this patient it's tailor-made.' He held out his hand. 'I apologise for being rude about your sister's remedies. I admit they have a limited usefulness. But not for Philomena. She has a childlike mind, and she is going to be a mother. I told her nothing can do any good for her now except to get out and about, try to settle in some bedsit and get the social services to visit.'

Robyn was curt. 'Paul—her wound has opened up again.'

'God, no! You mean she's done it herself? How could you let it happen?'

Robyn sighed. 'I can't be everywhere at once, you know. But I know she's done it because she's terrified of being sent home.'

Paul stood for a moment. He didn't apologise, but he did say, 'Perhaps I shouldn't have spoken to her like that just yet.'

Realising that he was only doing his best for the poor girl, Robyn said, 'She isn't an easy patient.'

Paul turned and looked directly into Robyn's eyes. 'Thanks for that. Are we friends?'

She smiled as they shook hands, and said, 'I'm glad you asked that. Now I can invite you to dinner.'

'That's very civil of you, Bobbie.' And he didn't let her take her hand away for a moment, as he looked into her eyes. 'I'd like to accept very much.'

'The thirtieth?'

'I'll have to check my diary. Anyone else invited?'

'Ross Cartwright,' she said with a smile.

'Ah——'

'You could tell him how much more tolerant and open-minded you are.'

Paul let her hand go, and picked up his coffee-mug. 'I forgot. I'm going to London that weekend. There's something on at the Hammersmith. I really am sorry.'

'Of course.' Naturally he would spend his weekends with his girlfriend; and naturally, too, he wouldn't want to share the limelight at the Wests' cottage with another personable young man. 'Some other time, perhaps.'

'Yes, sure.' He picked up the phone. 'Bleep Tony, would you? He ought to have been here by now!' And he set off round the ward, speaking now only of the patients. The breathless houseman and Robyn followed with the appropriate notes, Robyn with a feeling of emptiness inside. Just as they seemed to be growing closer, Robyn had been well and truly reminded not to entertain any romantic notions about Paul Howell-Jones. He was only here to do a job. Why, if he were thinking of staying in Barnaby, he would already be looking for a house to buy, instead of living in the hospital accommodation. No, his heart was still quite obviously in the south, and Robyn and Chase Hey were merely diversions in a London-based high-tech, high-speed life.

They returned to the office, where Paul gave her some instructions about drugs and treatment. Just as he was leaving he stopped and added, 'And you can tell Sally that lavender is very good for anxiety and palpitations, if the patchouli doesn't work.' And he winked.

'Sarcastic so-and-so.' He didn't believe a word of the book. He'd been pulling her leg. Robyn tried to be cool and calm. 'One day, Doctor, you are going to need some of our mumbo-jumbo very badly—and you'll be sorry you spoke so slightingly of it.'

'You aren't casting a spell on me, are you, Robyn?'

'Don't be so supercilious, please.'

'I didn't mean any harm.' His face was open now. 'Only joking. I am really sorry about the thirtieth.' He picked up his stethoscope and shoved it into the pocket of his white coat. 'And you do look beautiful when you're angry.' He was gone. Robyn tried not to think of him and his infuriating ways, but again it became impossible to get the memory of his kisses out of her mind.

It was Friday, which was the twenty-ninth. As Robyn waved to Mary as she drove out of the path in the morning, Mary called after her, 'And I almost forgot! Dinner is tonight. Ross didn't mind changing the date so that Paul can come along too.'

Robyn banged her foot on the brake. 'You might have told me earlier.'

'You wouldn't have let me change the date.'

'I probably wouldn't. Mary——' She wound the window down fully, and waited while Mary wheeled herself towards the car. 'You know I don't get on awfully well with Paul, don't you? He doesn't belong in Barnaby. Oh, he's nice enough to everyone, but his heart isn't here, and it shows. We've had more words.'

'Not again.'

'He's nice as pie to you, but he goes round making fun of us all the same.'

'He doesn't mean it. He doesn't do it behind your back, you know. And he's been to the shop and actually bought some of Jackie's stuff. I think you're being supersensitive about him, honestly.'

'I'll try to be polite tonight.'

'Thank you. It'll be a lovely meal. And we could sit outside in the moonlight for coffee and liqueurs. The roses smell divine, especially the King's Ransom. I'm looking forward to it very much.'

And Robyn was again alerted by something in Mary's voice. 'You like Ross, don't you, Mary?'

'Yes, I do.'

Robyn nodded. 'I'm a selfish pig, thinking only of myself. I'm not delighted that you invited Paul, but I promise I'll take him for a stroll in the shrubbery so that you can have a few moments together.'

'I'd appreciate that, Sis.'

'The West sisters entertain! Watch this space! See you, Mary.' And she drove off to Chase Hey, glad that at last Mary had met someone she liked, and was doing something positive about it. Ross was a genuine, likeable man, and Robyn was determined to promote his friendship with Mary, even though it meant she had to be partnered with Paul. Still, it was a good cause. And Paul would most likely have his thoughts on London, and wouldn't think of repeating his over-affectionate behaviour of the night of the dinner.

The ward was buzzing with conversation when she went in. 'Sister, haven't you heard? Mr Black has come off his horse. He was riding with Willy Bragg. They say he cracked his skull, but how could he if he was wearing a hard hat? He's having emergency surgery right now!' Robyn stood as if stunned, until the sound of little Philomena weeping in sympathy with Mr Black called her back to her duties.

CHAPTER FOUR
July

THE dinner party at Meadow Cottage, along with many other events that day, had been delayed by the bad news. The weekend had passed, with much drama over the councillor's riding accident. He was in Intensive Care for almost a week, before Mr Sarmsworth, the surgeon, declared him out of danger. There was much speculation over where he should be treated. But Chase Hey was the logical place, the closest to his home, and Claude Sarmsworth was one of the most experienced surgeons in the area. As the chairman lay helpless in Chase Hey Hospital, Robyn was only one of many who prayed that this unfortunate accident would prove to him how essential the hospital was, and how tragic it would be to close it down.

Only when the alarm was over did Mary West finally manage to bring herself and her sister together with Paul and Ross for the proposed dinner party. She was charmingly open about it as they sat on the patio drinking wine, looking at the sunset, and smelling the new roses. 'I realised that the chances don't come along every day for someone like me, who spends a lot of time in the house. So I made life come to me! I do hope you don't mind. I've cooked a goose for you.'

Paul handed her a small box. 'I do hope that doesn't apply to our campaign, Mary! A cooked goose! But thank you for asking me, and this little gift is for you.

49

Though, for someone with your talents in a garden, it seems very small and insignificant.'

Mary opened the little box, and took out a perfect pink orchid, decked with fern, and wrapped in silver. 'Paul, how exquisite! I've always wanted to be given an orchid.'

Paul handed another box to Robyn. 'And for you, Bobbie.' He lowered his voice, so that only Robyn could hear. 'I tried to get one the colour of moonlight.'

Robyn was annoyed with herself for not keeping the emotion out of her face at the sight of the milky, translucent flower. A thoughtful gift, from someone who was so very far from perfect himself, but still had the ability to bring tears into her voice. Annoyed with herself for showing emotion, she said huskily, 'Thank you, Paul.'

Ross Cartwright had been watching the girls' reactions. He said, 'I suppose I can't live up to that for romance, girls, but I thought champagne might stimulate us all to work for success in the campaign.' And he unwrapped the bottle that had been concealed, not very successfully, at his side. 'I thought perhaps we could get together and drink it when we had won.'

Mary took it with grateful thanks. 'I'm touched. I'll keep it chilled, Ross. I'm sure it won't be long before we do win.'

Robyn noticed that Paul was going to interrupt at this comment, but he leaned back, changing his mind. She was pleased, because it showed he was learning how to be less pushy, less inclined to dominate the conversation. She smiled at him, showing him she had noticed his tact, before saying, 'I suppose we must keep optimistic, Mary. But things don't look so rosy any more. It's Mr Black, you see. When he was thrown from his horse he fell on his head. He was wearing a helmet, but the strap broke, and he hit some rocks.'

'I heard that.' Ross was watching her. 'But he was operated on in Chase Hey. Surely that has to be good for you?'

Paul agreed. 'Ought to have been. The trouble is, we don't have a modern CT scanner. He had to go into the neuro unit in town for assessment before he was transferred here.'

'Oh, dear. He won't be pleased about that.' Mary grasped the situation quickly. 'He's already complained that Chase Hey would be taking money better used for modern equipment in the city hospital.Now he'll be even more against us.'

Paul said, 'If he knew. But when I left the ward today he hadn't regained consciousness.'

'I'm so sorry. I thought he was out of danger.' Mary was always concerned about patients, understandably, having been through so much herself. And Mr Black was a patient who could have done them a lot of good.

Paul went on, 'He is. Physically he's getting better. He got the best surgical attention possible after the scan had been done. But it doesn't alter the fact that the essential investigations couldn't be done here.'

Robyn sipped her wine rather sadly, before adding, 'Nothing can change the facts. I suppose now the whole campaign is near to hopeless, Paul? I had hoped—lots of us had—that he would realise how much this area needs Chase Hey. Of all people to have in Ward Eleven, it has to be the chairman of the district health authority. And unconscious! No one can possibly guess what he'll think of us after all this is over.'

Paul turned to her, his handsome face grave. 'The

tests showed no abnormality. He's had a bad shock, a broken clavicle, a cracked skull and a twisted knee. He's also had the best possible treatment, and he ought to be grateful for it. But he's known as an awkward fellow, we all know that. He's a lucky man to be alive, from what I hear of that horse.'

Ross Cartwright intervened. 'One of Bragg's, was it? I hope they didn't give him Napoleon—he's an unpredictable brute. We've had a story about Napoleon in the *Recorder* before, and Bragg had to promise he wouldn't be hired out as a hack any more.'

Paul seized on the remark. 'If that horse is a danger to the public then maybe the fact that our equipment is more out-of-date than City's might be played down. The blame for Black's condition isn't ours but Willy Bragg's.'

Robyn shook her head. 'Surely it makes no difference, Paul? We still didn't have the facilities he needed.'

'But we have the surgical team, Robyn—and it was easy enough to ambulance him over for the scan. You don't want me to give up, do you, after only four months in the job? This is a set-back—not the clapper of doom!'

Ross Cartwright actually smiled. 'I like the sound of it, Paul! A man of conviction, are you, or just someone who hates to lose?'

'Both, if I'm honest. No one will believe that I'm here because I care about the place, even though Barnaby is growing on me. So just think of me as a winner, OK?'

Ross said, 'I want to, believe me. It would do the paper a lot of good, too, to have a part in saving Chase Hey. So has anyone got an angle for me? Robyn said we could talk about it. You think it would serve any purpose, pointing out Napoleon's bad character? Implicating Willy Bragg? I'd have to check the facts, of course.'

Mary's quiet voice interrupted at that point. 'Chilled cucumber and watercress soup in the dining-room. Shall we go on with this discussion over dinner?'

Much later, as they sat on the patio drinking Columbian coffee, their conversation much livelier than before the meal, Robyn looked across at Mary, and nodded slightly. 'Time I showed Paul the herbaceous border. All unbelievers should be initiated in the art of herbalism in July, when all the plants are doing so well and smell so—so healthy!'

Paul protested. 'What unbelievers? You know I've been reading one of Jackie's books!' But he stood up quite rapidly all the same. 'When I buy my house in Barnaby I'll need to know what grows well around here. Who better to teach me than the West sisters?'

He said 'when' not 'if'. Paul living in Barnaby. He had never mentioned anything about buying a house before. It sounded good. Robyn led the way round the crazy-paved path beside the raspberry canes that shielded the garden from the cottage. Paul pulled at her hand. 'Why are you trying to run away from me?' His grip was strong, and his intentions obvious.

Robyn looked up at him, the warm, masculine shape of him outlined against the stars. It had been such a happy evening, in spite of their worries about their future. Now it was her responsibility to keep Paul amused, while Ross was given the chance to get to know Mary better. Robyn said, 'I think you know the answer to that.' She stepped in front of him, edging herself past his desirable frame with one quick step.

'And now we'll take an educational stroll along the thyme and chickory beds.'

His voice was low but decisive. 'The hell we will! Herbs are OK in their place. But midnight in a perfumed garden with a beautiful woman is not one of those places.' He had placed himself immediately in front of her again. Robyn knew very well that her resistance was low. She didn't realise just how much she had yearned for his physical nearness, and how quickly she would reach out at his first touch, and draw him into her arms with a need as strong as his. After the first strenuous and passionate embrace she managed to whisper, 'I'm doing this for Mary, you know.'

He kissed her then, and it was a long, complicated and emotional experience, as Paul overcapped his previous performance, holding her with strong arms, taking her mouth with hungry tongue and lips, deep breathing, and whispered sweet words that Robyn couldn't believe were meant for her. 'Do it for Mary again, darling.'

She tried to pull away. 'Paul, please. . .'

'You're afraid of me.' He moved fractionally away, allowing her to catch her breath. 'I don't want that. I want you to want what I want. So the moment you tell me to go back to the house. . .' His voice was teasing.

'Don't be cruel. You know I want them to have some time together.'

Paul let her go then, and smiled at her in the moonlight as she backed away quickly and leaned as casually as possible against a pear-tree trunk. 'You think I'm cruel?'

'Well—no, not really. But you must know what I mean. I wanted——'

'You wanted Ross and Mary to be alone. But what

you didn't realise, my innocent, is that Ross Cartwright is falling for you, not Mary. Every minute we stay out here, he gets more and more agitated—I might just ravish you between the celandines and the basil.' He came towards her, but only briefly to touch her forehead with his lips. 'For both their sakes, we ought to go back, even though for ours—for mine—we ought to stay here.'

Robyn looked up at him, incredulous. 'But how can you possibly know that? Ross made no sign—he didn't even talk to me much. Are you sure you know what you're talking about?'

'Very sure. I know a jealous man when I see one.'

Robyn dropped her hands to her sides, and sighed. 'Oh, dear. Poor Mary.' She looked at Paul again. 'We'll go back, then.'

Paul said, 'We'd better. Ross hates my guts, and it isn't about the hospital, or about my style of leadership. It's about Robyn West.'

They began to walk back silently, the nightingale trilling in the pear tree. She said, trying to bring the conversation back to normality, 'This business of Black could really be very bad for us, couldn't it? You were only saying brave words because you wanted to keep our spirits up?'

'I suppose so, Bobbie.' His voice was resigned, honest. 'But you're not to say so. Not to anyone else. Sometimes it's very important to keep up appearances. Will you promise? I don't want to have to lead a dispirited army.'

'I'll do my best.'

'Thanks.' He stopped, and tilted her face to look at him. She felt very close to him at that moment, although they were scarcely touching. He said, 'I wish——'

'What?'

'Oh, nothing. Only for life to be straightforward. I like happy endings.' His deep voice was sad, his face shadowed in the moonlight.

Robyn felt a strong desire to comfort him. But she fought it. However close they had been tonight, however much of his private self he had revealed to her, she had to remember that Paul belonged to London, and to Victoria Alexander. Her own future lay here, with Chase Hey. All the same, their sudden embrace was mutual and passionate, she was no longer afraid, and again she felt those tendrils of frustrated desire unfold and fill her being, body and soul with a great need of him.

Next morning, as she got ready to drive into town for groceries, Mary was washing lettuce and tomatoes from the greenhouse. 'You think the dinner went well?'

Robyn had tried not to mention it. Now she said, 'It was a splendid meal. Your guests surely praised you enough, didn't they?'

'Oh, yes. But the hospital, the campaign? Do you think we got the two men to like each other more?'

'I think so. I'm sure of it.' Paul had told her to be positive, and she had promised to try.

'Did Paul kiss you?'

Robyn stopped at the door and turned in surprise. 'Why do you want to know?'

'I think you suit one another.'

Robyn pretended to be counting out the coins in her purse. She gave a brief nod. 'See you soon.' And she drove away without looking back. Robyn felt mean, knowing that Ross liked her more than Mary, as though she were cheating the sister she was supposed to protect. Life had been so much easier before the arrival in Barnaby of Dr Howell-Jones, and the awakening of those tendrils that curled round her heart and reminded her how painful and powerful love could be.

At work on Monday Paul was in the ward almost before Robyn. He waited while she quickly went round the beds, chatting to her patients, and making sure she knew how they were. This morning she was acutely conscious of him standing in her office, a brooding figure in his clean white coat, waiting for her. She knew too that the physical power of Friday's encounter still filled her with genuine need. Mrs Wood sat up in bed as Robyn came to her. 'You look pretty today, Sister.'

Robyn was startled. Mrs Wood never thought about anyone but herself. Was her depression lifting at last? 'Thank you. You sound bright and breezy.'

'It's that nice Dr Howell-Jones. Changed me tablets, he did. And Sally took me to the physio and showed me some exercises.'

Back in her room, Robyn tried to joke, 'You've cured Mrs Wood, Paul. You and Sally, the disbelievers. And Philomena is a lot less nervy—hasn't touched her bandages. I feel that at last I'm getting somewhere.'

'I think maybe we are—together.' But his voice was grave. 'Robyn, the committee think perhaps we should cancel the garden party out of respect for Swainson Black. What do you think?'

'Cancel? It would mean refunding a lot of ticket money. But perhaps—money isn't everything. Is the councillor no better?'

'Still in a coma.'

Robyn picked up a pile of letters, leafed through them absently. 'He might come round today. You said we must stay optimistic.'

Paul nodded. He seemed reluctant to get on with his work. 'Thanks again for the dinner.'

'Mary's. I didn't do much.'

'Maybe you did more than you think.' His eyes were on her, and, as she looked up, she was impressed by the brooding fire in them, which somehow matched her own smouldering feelings. 'I wanted to say—I mean—maybe it's love-your-enemy time, Bobbie? Come out with me tonight?'

'You know that's out of the question.'

'I don't see how.'

'Then you're very insensitive.'

'Robyn, sweet——'

'Don't ever call me that!' She stood up, and the sheaf of papers fell to the floor, scattering in all directions. Paul bent to help her pick them up, and for a moment their heads were very close together.

He stopped with a few letters in his hand, and looked into her eyes. 'Why not? I'm only human, you know.'

Robyn sank back on her heels amid the papers. 'You've been here almost four months. Only another eight to go. I know you joked about buying a house, but I know better. After this, you'll be back to Victoria and to London. That's why. I don't want to be a temporary toy, Paul. It isn't in my nature.'

Paul bent and swept up the papers fiercely, shuffling them into a neat pile, and standing up to put them on her desk with a bang. As Robyn scrambled up beside him, he muttered, 'Let's go and cure a few patients, then.' And with white coat flying after him like wings, he strode from the office and straight to the first bed, while Robyn scrabbled hastily for the patient's notes, and followed him, out of breath and pink-cheeked with the effort and with embarrassment.

They completed the ward-round in a strictly businesslike way, saying nothing unnecessary. As the round proceeded Robyn began to feel very angry with him, for making her feel guilty, when he was the one who had been making immoral suggestions. The houseman, Tony, caught up with them, and thankfully Robyn was able to stand next to him, not to Paul, whose very warmth and closeness set off those physical reactions she was getting very used to lately, the beating heart and sweating palms, the inner yearnings.

She again admired his gentle treatment of Philomena. 'I hear you had a scan, and that your baby is doing well?'

'Yes, Doctor.' But the small face was serious. 'I didn't think it was real before.'

'And now you know you'll be a real mum?'

Philomena whispered, 'Yes.' But there were tears in her eyes because there was no real dad beside her.

Robyn bent and said briskly, 'We'll have a nice chat soon. You mustn't worry about anything. I'm here, remember?'

As Tony stood with Paul in her office, discussing therapy, Paul looked up and said casually, 'No coffee today, Sister?'

Still angry with him for making her feel like the guilty one, she filled her kettle, and plugged it in with a harder than necessary twist on the wrist. There was no conversation as they drank their coffee, and Tony eyed them both warily, before making himself scarce. It was unheard-of for Sister West to get in a mood.

'We can let Mrs Wood go home tomorrow, Robyn.' His attractive, gravelly voice was cool. 'I'll see her weekly in Out-patients at first, to keep up the reassurance she needs.'

'I'll arrange it.' She took the file from him, and made the note. There was none of the exhilaration she ought to have felt at persuading an unbeliever to use traditional herbs instead of chemicals. They were having their first real row, and it made her very miserable indeed.

He waited until she looked up. Then he said, 'I'll not ask again. I can see how you feel. If you change your mind—I'll be waiting.' And he put down the treatment book, and turned to leave.

At that moment the phone rang, and Robyn picked it up. It was Ward Eleven. 'Is Dr Howell-Jones with you, Robyn?'

'Yes—do you want to speak to him?'

'No. Just let him know that Mr Swainson Black has regained consciousness, and is fully orientated.'

Robyn replaced the receiver, her mood lightening a little. She actually smiled at Paul as she repeated the message. 'We're not finished after all. The garden party is still on, then. We've still got a chance. We must take it, treat him with kid gloves.'

'A chance? So we have.' The double meaning was quite clear in his eyes, as they lost their steeliness, and softened as he looked at her. 'Will you come with me?'

'But——'

'I'm not making a pass at you, woman. I just want someone from the committee to accompany me, OK?'

She said, trying to sound adult, 'That will be all right, then. But I'll have to bring Mary too.'

'As chaperon?'

'No, because she has no one else to bring her.'

'What about that Jackie woman? Aren't they buddies?'

'Colleagues, yes.'

'Then ask Jackie.'

Robyn faced him and looked up into his face. 'I couldn't do that,' she said flatly. 'I'd never dump Mary like some unwanted luggage. You should have gathered that by now.'

Paul shrugged. 'I can't understand how the poor kid could have caught polio in this day and age. Don't tell me your parents were daft enough to believe in herbs too!'

Robyn's voice was dignified and quiet as she explained, 'We moved around a lot when we were young. Daddy was a missionary. I guess she just missed getting her booster injection because we were setting off for Mombasa that day. Mother wasn't very well at the time. She died out there.'

There was a silence. Outside the window they could hear a lark in full-throated song rising against a clear blue sky, and the backcloth of Willy Bragg's horses in a smooth green field. Paul Howell-Jones looked down at his own feet, before looking back at Robyn, and saying, 'I'm very sorry. I was disgustingly rude. It's unforgivable of me.' And he turned on his heel, and left the room.

His humility had a strange effect on Robyn. Again she wanted to reach out and hold him, reassure him that she wasn't offended. As the door swung to she ran and opened it again. Paul was striding down the corridor, his athletic step taking him further from her when she wanted him to stop and listen to her pardoning his rudeness. Without meaning to, she called out, 'Paul!'

The corridor was deserted. He stopped, and turned. She thought how handsome he was, his broad shoulders emphasised by the white coat, his face and jaw sculpted and elegant in the light from the window. 'Yes?'

Robyn went to him, her knees feeling peculiarly shaky. She stopped within a yard of him. Why had she called him back?

What was it she wanted to say to him? 'I'm sorry. It was impulsive of me. I shouldn't have called you back. You're a busy man.'

'I didn't come back. I waited. What did you want to tell me?'

'Just—just—if you go to see Mr Black, please give him my good wishes. . . And thank you for being so tactful with Philomena. I think it means a lot to her.' She watched him stride away, knowing how much she wanted to say a whole lot of things that would be quite useless and totally undignified.

CHAPTER FIVE
August

VERY much aware now of her feelings towards Paul, Robyn found that by being honest with herself she was able to control her surges of emotion, and rationalise them by telling herself firmly that she was a frustrated old maid making herself ridiculous over a man who could never belong to her except on his own terms—those terms being purely temporary, and for his own convenience. All the same, she would lie in bed some nights, staring at the moonlight on the ceiling, and wonder why she was holding out, when even Paul's terms would give her some brief happiness.

The warm summer had given way, suddenly, to a spell of rain. As a gardener, Mary was delighted with the extra watering her vegetables were getting. 'Just look at those runner-beans, Bobbie! Have we ever seen them so long and plump?'

'Long runner-beans won't save the garden party, though.'

Mary was as sunny as the day was grey. 'Don't worry! The arcade is almost finished. We can put the stalls inside. And have you ever known Barnaby people miss a party just because of the weather? We all have umbrellas, you know.'

'I suppose you're right.'

'Don't sound so miserable, Bobbie. What are you wearing?'

Robyn shrugged. 'Paul suggests that all the women

go over the top and pretend they're going to Ladies' Day at Ascot!'

'That's a great idea. All the more pictures for Ross!'

'Ross has guaranteed us a page, has he?'

'More than that. He's picking me up, Bobbie. You don't. . .mind—do you?'

The sun came out for Robyn then. 'He is? How marvellous! Have you been seeing him without telling me?'

'Not really. He pops in if he's passing. He's so sweet, you know, the way he has become so keen on our campaign. By the way, has Paul dropped his opposition to the arcade?'

Robyn said with some sarcasm, 'Paul never drops anything. He's like a bull terrier. But he was outvoted. The committee are in favour of anything that brings in the cash!'

'Really? Then he won't mind having a festival in the hospital grounds next month?'

Robyn knew her sister well enough to look wary. 'What sort of festival? Even the committee don't want hordes of screaming teenagers and unwashed guitar-players making ghastly noises that would ruin our patients' hearing.'

'Tell you later. Go and get ready!'

It had rained in the night, but the morning of the Garden Party promised a glimmer of sun through rosy clouds. Robyn tried on her best full-skirted rose-printed organdie—and found that it was too big round the waist. 'You've not been eating properly, Bobbie. I told you!'

Robyn said nothing, aware herself of how her appetite had diminished since she'd fallen in love. 'What can we do about it?'

'A large wide belt. Quite sexy, really. Are you going to wear a hat?' The girls rummaged in wardrobes and drawers, and found a white belt Robyn had last worn at a Scout dance as a young teenager. She decided against a hat, as her shining hair was too soft and the hat kept slipping off. Mary had an idea. 'Make the dress's own belt into a ribbon. Here, give it to me.' She snipped the end from the self-belt, and quickly fashioned a rose shape which she stitched to a hair-grip. 'There, isn't that pretty?'

Robyn had to admit she looked quite dishy. 'And it's in a good cause, mutton dressed as lamb.'

'Don't you dare mention your age! You look like a film star—and I don't mean Lassie.'

The first gleams of real sunlight filtered through the pear-tree leaves as Ross Cartwright presented himself at the front door of Meadow Cottage. Mary was still in her bedroom, and Robyn opened the door to him. 'Hi, Robyn. I say, you look good enough to eat.' He sat down when invited. He was wearing a smart enough shirt, no jacket, and jeans. But it suited him. Ross wasn't the dressing-up type, and would have looked starchy and uncomfortable in a suit. He went on, 'Chase Hey mustn't close, Robyn. Barnaby wouldn't be the same without the beautiful West sisters. And Mary tells me you would have to move on—get a job in a city hospital?'

Robyn nodded, feeling miserable at the thought. Surely it couldn't happen. She looked around, at the floral chairs, comfortable sofa, the cosy home-made rug, the battered old piano in the corner, and the pretty curtains of Meadow Cottage's living-room. 'It would be a big decision.'

Ross was looking at her, not the furniture. 'A

tragedy.' There was something in those eyes—warm brown, with a hint of ginger in them, just like his hair—that reminded Robyn of Paul's warning. 'It's you he wants, not Mary. . .' Robyn changed the subject quickly. 'You wouldn't know what kind of festival wants to hire the hospital grounds, would you, Ross?'

He grinned. 'You mean the Holy Enlightenment College?'

'The Holy *what*?'

Ross's smile grew wider, and his eyes twinkled. 'Thought you believed in meditation, Robyn.'

'Hey, let's get this clear. I use meditation to help calm nervous patients. But I use medication too. Doesn't this sect believe in allowing God to heal the patient through prayer alone? We couldn't have that in a hospital—could we?'

'Their money is good, I believe—some trillionaire from Nepal backs them. In fact, I'd say a two-day festival would almost get you to your target.'

Mary wheeled herself in then. 'I heard that. You told her, Ross!' She was dressed in a glamorous tunic and slim trousers of emerald and blue figured silk, and her pretty hair fluffed round her face and shoulders. Robyn felt that Ross Cartwright would be blind not to think Mary the more beautiful of the West sisters. She had often wondered what would happen if they both fell for the same man. Would she stand aside for Mary's sake?

Ross was looking too. 'Wow!' Mary looked pleased. He said, 'Well, I'm honoured to be driving you both. Shall we go?'

Robyn saw he had misunderstood. Quickly she said,

'Come on, Mary, I'll give you a hand with the chair. I'll follow along later, when I'm ready.'

'You're not coming with us?' She could tell he was disappointed. She hoped Mary couldn't, in the flurry of helping her into the front seat, and folding the chair into the boot.

'See you in a few minutes!' But her heart sank as Paul's scarlet Lotus drew up before Ross had time to move away from the cottage gate. Robyn saw Ross's eyes in the driving-mirror. His face was set and grave, and she felt a pang of guilt.

Paul was opening the door for Robyn. She got in with a murmured greeting, still thoughtful. Suddenly Paul leaned over, and kissed her cheek briefly. 'Hey— I'm here!'

She looked at him then. 'I'm sorry. I was thinking.'

'You've heard about the Holy Enlightenment College! I can't think what else would make you look so preoccupied!'

She smiled. 'I've heard. What do you think, Paul?'

He put the Lotus in gear, and they roared away after Ross's station wagon towards the hospital. 'No chance at all. We've enough weirdos with your sister's lot in the arcade. That's as far as I'm prepared to go.'

Robyn had been against the idea herself, but Paul's blunt antagonism made her bridle. 'You don't know what they believe in yet. And they're paying good money, Paul. Ross thinks we'd be more than halfway to our target if we take them. It is only for two days.'

'Ross wants us to look ridiculous, does he?'

Robyn said calmly, 'That's for the committee to decide—not Ross, and not you or me.'

'Oh, really?' His tone was sharp. She looked at him as they parked in the space reserved for consultants.

He unwound his elegant legs from the sports car, and stood, a superb figure in light grey suit, handsome and strong, a man who seemed capable of taking on the world. Their eyes met. He walked round, and held out his hand to help her from her seat. 'Why are we arguing, Bobbie?'

'I think maybe it's become a habit.'

He still held her hand, staring down at her, their looks interlocked. 'I think I'm drowning in your eyes.' His deep voice was almost a whisper.

She knew that if she answered him with equally tender words she would be lost. Yet the sweetness of the moment brought a pain to her heart, an unwanted tear to her eye, and he noticed it, and gently wiped it away with his forefinger. She had to take the situation in hand at once. Clearing her throat, she said swiftly, 'I think it's time to go and make some money!'

'Sure.' He let go of her hand while he locked the car and put on the alarm electronically. Then he held out his arm, and she put her hand in the crook of his elbow. She felt proud, and confident, to be escorted by such a man, knowing that heads turned as they walked past towards the stalls and the main stage, where microphones were being tested, and a brass band was getting itself into position.

Tom Gordon was talking to John Crabtree. He came to meet the couple. 'I say, you make a handsome pair! We were just deciding who would pop up to Ward Eleven to take some flowers to Councillor Swainson Black. You've just won, Dr Howell-Jones and Sister West! Would you mind?'

'Not at all.' Paul took the bouquet, and placed it in Robyn's arms, while he picked up the Good Wishes card and a box containing a commemorative gold tiepin. 'He'll know we're buttering him up. But it's in a good cause—and if I were Black I'd feel a heap better at the sight of Sister West in that dress, wouldn't you?'

'You look a picture,' confirmed John Crabtree, with a wink at Robyn.

They went into the quiet and cool of Chase Hey together, the scent of the roses in the bouquet masking the hospital smell of disinfectant and last night's dinner. The Councillor was sitting up, listening to the distant brass band. His face brightened at the sight of his visitors. 'And I thought I'd be missing the fun.' He was very grateful, but Robyn could see that he was far from well. They stayed with him only a few minutes, before Paul decided he had had enough.

'You'd better get some rest, Councillor.' And, outside the ward, Paul shook his head. 'There's something wrong. His personality seems to have changed. He looks worried all the time. So much older.'

'But to come round from a coma and be all right—surely he'll recover, given time?'

Paul didn't answer, and Robyn knew that was because the answer was unknown. They didn't speak until they came out again into the sunshine. Then he looked at her, and said with a twinkle, 'Won't you take my arm again? I like being close to you.'

She pretended reluctance. 'I suppose I must.'

But at that moment there came a shout from the end of the corridor. 'Is that you, Robyn?'

She turned. Sally, also in party dress, was running towards her. 'It's Philomena. They asked me to find you. I think she's losing the baby. Could you come? They've sent for the obstetrician.'

Paul looked from one to the other. 'I'll come along too.' As they hurried along the cool corridor, he went on, 'I thought having that child was going to settle her down, Robyn. God knows how she'll take this. Just as we got her arm healed up nicely.'

The little patient wasn't in the ward. Tony said, 'They've taken her to Theatre, Robyn. They said not to disturb her just now. But she asked if you'd see her later.'

'So she lost the child?'

'Yes, it's a D and C.'

Robyn grimaced in disappointment. 'In one way I'm glad she isn't going to be a one-parent family. But in another, I was beginning to think that having someone of her own to love would help her grow up.'

Paul said quietly, 'You have become her family, you know. The baby would have helped to wean her away from here. But—we can't win 'em all.' He put his hand gently round Robyn's waist. 'Come on. We can't do any good here just now.' And they made their way across the rapidly drying grass. Paul put his other hand over hers and squeezed it. She protested, trying to regain the light-hearted party mood, that people would talk. 'I have my reputation to think of in Barnaby!'

'And I have mine, my dear. Always to be the companion of the best-looking woman at the party!'

'Any party?'

'Most certainly. And don't you go straying away while I'm making my speech of welcome, young lady!' In the middle of their joking and laughing he suddenly leaned over and murmured in her ear. 'You're part of my life now, Bobbie, whether you like it or not.'

His words burned into her soul. The band played lustily, fashionable dresses and tailored suits mingled with jeans and T-shirts, and the sun beamed down hotter on the striped stalls as noon approached. Paul and Robyn stood together, and noticed none of this, as poor Robyn found her determination not to get involved gradually and positively ebbing away. She said, trying to stay cool and detached from his real meaning, 'One's colleagues at work do tend to become rather like members of one's family.'

'Don't deliberately misunderstand me, my dear. You know exactly what I'm saying.' His hand was very warm and protective over hers as she clung on to his arm, knowing that by the end of today the combination of his sensuous voice and his beautiful words would have won her over totally and completely. Their shared concern about Philomena had been the final strand that completed her certainty. She felt a tingle of excitement at having finally decided to give in to Paul's entreaties. The tendrils started to unwind and grow. . .

But at that moment a very penetrating, languid female voice interrupted their tête-à-tête, and Paul's fingers tensed over Robyn's. 'So this is where you got to, Paul, darling! We've been looking simply everywhere for you, haven't we, Fiona?'

With a muffled expletive, Paul disentangled himself from Robyn, and turned to face Victoria Alexander with a sudden forced delight. 'What a super surprise, Vicki. Fiona, how nice of you to come and support our little efforts.' His voice had changed completely from the gentle husky caressing tones he had been using on Robyn. He kissed the two ravishing models with effusive bonhomie. Robyn didn't stay to be introduced. Thankful that she was well acquainted with all the nooks and crannies of Chase Hey gardens, she slipped behind the main tent, and across a small lawn into the shadow of the trees. She looked at her fingers—still pink from the pressure of Paul Howell-Jones's guilty grip. Thank goodness those girls had turned up, just in time to stop her making a complete ass of herself. It would never happen again. Robyn West wasn't the sort of girl to put herself in such a situation twice!

She found a wooden seat. The band had stopped playing, and the crackle of the microphone and then muffled, echoing words indicated that the garden party was being officially declared open. In a minute it would be Paul's turn to speak. Robyn found that she was crying. Even though she had seen him slip back into his London ways, his upper-class voice, she still loved him very much. Physically his closeness for the past hour or two had begun to work its magic on her again, and she felt the desperate, empty longing that she had started to recognise the first time Paul had kissed her.

But, deep down, she was a Barnaby lass, and Barnaby lasses didn't waste time crying over spilt milk. Thank goodness she hadn't put any mascara on. She wiped the last of the tears, and waited, her sadness turning moment by moment into anger and determination, until the redness had gone from her face. Checking in her handbag mirror, she walked back towards the throng, making her way to the opposite side of the grounds from the main tent.

'Why, Robyn, how glamorous you look.' 'Hi, Robyn, nice to see you!' 'Over here, love, we haven't had a chat for ages.' She was among friends, and soon her mood had lifted, as she responded to the warmth of the people, and also delighted in the numbers who had turned up, counting their ticket money in her head, and reflecting that this must be one of their most successful attempts to raise the money they needed for the campaign. She looked over at the squat grey building that was Chase Hey. It looked so permanent in the sunshine, its lovely grounds well-tailored for the occasion. How could they possibly let it die?

Philomena would be out of Theatre by now. Careless of the festivities now, Robyn retraced her steps back to the hospital and her own ward. She asked Staff Nurse on duty if Philomena was back. 'No, Robyn. But apparently she asked if she could come here instead of staying in a strange ward.'

'I'll talk to them.' Robyn sat at her desk, her pretty skirt flowing round her legs, and the beribboned hair-grip falling unheeded on to the floor. She picked up the phone. 'Yes, I'm on duty until she's OK. I'd like to be here for her.'

Though she was still drowsy from the anaesthetic Philomena's face lit up when she saw Robyn. 'You look like a princess, Sister.'

There had been no time to explain to her what had happened. Robyn said, 'Have a long sleep, love, and we'll talk tomorrow.'

'I know the baby's died.'

'I'm afraid it has.'

'Was it a little boy or a little girl?'

'A girl, Phil.'

Sleepily she answered, 'Then maybe she's better off than me where she is. She might not have liked growing up.' And she turned her face away, and closed her eyes. Robyn waited, with tears in her eyes, until regular breathing showed the girl was asleep.

She walked to the window. The crowded gardens seemed lively and happy. She caught sight of Paul's head, on a level with his two willowy female companions. They were making for the refreshment tent.

As they entered she noticed another striking figure,
dressed in a white robe and turban, chatting to Tom
Gordon. The Holy Enlightenment College chief!
Robyn gave a thoughtful smile. Paul was so set against
allowing this festival to go on. It would be suitable
punishment for him to find the rest of the committee
in favour of it! Making her way back to the gardens,
she systematically set about lobbying every member
who was there, persuading them how much they
needed the cash so thoughtfully offered by the Holy
Enlightenment College. Only when she knew she had
won did she allow her hunger pangs to drive her
towards the luncheon tables.

'Bobbie, where have you been all this time?' Mary
was sitting with Jackie Darcy in purple dungarees,
each with a half-pint of bitter. 'The beer's warm, but
it's welcome. Ross is around, taking pictures with his
photographer.'

Jackie tossed back a rope of twisted black hair. 'I
see your boyfriend has acquired a couple of dolly
girls.'

'Not boyfriend—just consultant on my ward.'
Robyn's face was composed, as she could see Mary
looking anxiously for signs of distress. 'And as far as
I'm concerned, those three deserve one another.'

Jackie said smugly, 'They've spent quite a lot on my
stuff, actually! And on the craft stall. Must be made of
money.'

Robyn was tart. 'I'm sure modelling pays a little
more than nursing. But if they've paid for their supper
then they're welcome to come again.'

She bought a salmon sandwich and a glass of white
wine. Jackie and Mary went back to the stalls, and for
a few moments Robyn sat alone in the bright open

tent, twirling the stem of her empty glass, grieving for Philomena's unnamed little child, for all the patients who would lose out if the hospital was closed, and wondering when it would be polite to go home.

Suddenly someone took the seat opposite, someone smelling of Chanel and body lotion, and dressed in slinky black with a low neckline, a string of chunky amethysts round a swan-like neck. 'It's Robyn, isn't it? Do you mind if I talk to you?'

'No, Victoria, I don't mind at all.' Robyn had a very good idea what this goddess wanted to say. 'Fire away.'

'I'd like you to stay away from Paul.'

'Shouldn't you tell that to him?'

'Not really. The poor dear is so easily distracted. And we're buying a flat together in Dulwich, so it would make things very unfortunate if he was side-tracked into backing out of his commitments in London. You do see what I'm getting at, sweetie?'

Robyn said quietly, 'I see, of course. But you're making a big mistake in coming to me. I give you my word I've no ambitions in Dr Howell-Jones's direction. I've given him no encouragement at all, and I can promise you I don't intend to. My mind is on other things just now, if you'll excuse me, Victoria.'

'I can't believe that, I'm afraid, sweetie. Don't forget what you were doing when Fiona and I arrived.'

'Very little. We'd linked arms, that's all. In fact, if you must know, we were discussing a patient.'

'You were extremely close together, and you were laughing and whispering as though you were having a jolly good time.'

Robyn gave her most ironic snort. 'It may be your idea of a good time, Victoria, but it isn't mine. As far as I'm concerned, Paul Howell-Jones is my consultant. He's also the chairman of the campaign we're running to save this hospital. I've never had a date with him, or even met him, on any other basis.'

Victoria Alexander looked into Robyn's face with large blue eyes ringed with azure shadow and navy blue eyelashes. 'I'm most terribly fond of Paul,' she said, and her voice trembled a little.

Robyn felt a twinge of sympathy. 'I can't see how someone as beautiful as you needs to worry. Any man would be a fool to prefer me to you.'

Victoria didn't seem comforted. 'Have you looked at yourself recently?'

'Yes—when I got dressed this morning.'

'And didn't you see anything?'

'Just a twenty-eight-year-old face.'

Victoria stood up. 'Give that twenty-eight-year-old face and body my make-up and clothes, and you'd not know yourself, sweetie. You could get any man you wanted—if you really wanted. So please—leave my man alone?'

'OK. No problem. Just make sure you tell him too!'

'I know my Paulie would be a good boy as long as he wasn't tempted.'

'I promise. No tempting. Cross my heart.'

Victoria nodded, her expression showing that she didn't know how seriously Robyn was taking this. 'OK, thanks, then.' As she wiggled away Robyn sat up straighter. A woman like that jealous of her! Of little Robyn West. Any man she wanted, eh? Sounded quite Mata Hari-ish. Someone came up behind her. 'Robyn, I want you to meet His Holiness.'

Robyn turned, to find the olive-skinned man in the

white turban alongside Tom Gordon. She smiled. 'How do you do?'

The Nepalese put his hands together in Indian greeting. 'Mr Gordon tells me you are in agreement for my followers to hold our festival of prayer and meditation in your beautiful grounds.'

Robyn said politely, 'I can't see anyone being offended by prayer and meditation, sir.'

'It is very kind of you to say so. I wonder——'

Robyn interrupted. 'Excuse me, but, although I agree, I'm afraid we are a committee, and we would need to have a meeting, and vote on the matter. If I introduce you to our chairman, it is up to him to decide when the meeting can take place.'

A large diamond flashed in the Nepalese turban. His Holiness's face was smooth and benign. How could Paul possibly object to such a gentle harmless creature? 'Your chairman is here?'

'I'll take you to him.'

'I shall be eternally grateful.'

Robyn looked around for Paul. He was laughing at something the dark girl, Fiona, was telling him, and Robyn remembered her anger at his fickleness, and led His Holiness straight to Paul, smiling secretly as she did so, aware that she had a majority on the committee who were in favour of taking the generous fee from the Holy Enlightenment College. 'Paul, I'm so sorry to bother you,' she said sweetly, 'but I'd like to introduce you to His Holiness. I have explained that the committee have to vote permission for his festival, but that I'm sure we would all be in favour!' And, as His Holiness gave Paul the *namaste* of folded hands, Robyn gave Paul, Fiona and Vicki her sweetest smile, and quietly made her getaway.

CHAPTER SIX
September

ROBYN and Mary West took their summer holiday as usual in the Lake District. It was calm and peaceful in the old stone farmhouse, and they spent a lot of time just chatting with the farmer's wife, watching the sheared sheep grazing, and sitting by the rippling river watching darting fish in the dappled shallows. Best of all, Robyn was away from Paul Howell-Jones's influence and disturbing presence, and had time to think logically about herself and her future.

On the riverbank, Robyn sat pensively. 'There's no question, Mary—saving the hospital is the most important thing we have to do. Without Chase Hey, I've no employment, and without my employment life would be hard for us. I have to work with Paul, and I have to get on with him.' She sighed. It wasn't going to get any easier.

'I know. Let's face it, I make my living with my herbs. If we had to move I'd lose my garden, and have to start from scratch somewhere else.' Mary pulled herself from her chair by means of a neighbouring branch, and stood for a moment, before trying a few faltering steps. She walked better with her calipers when they were alone, and she had no distractions. Clinging to the branch, she went on, 'I'd hate to leave the cottage, Bobbie, you know that. But if you have to, and if it comes to selling the cottage, then don't worry about me. Jackie said there's always room for a lodger at her place.'

Robyn's smile was wan. 'At least you'd get to stay in Barnaby, then. Can you see me in a drab nurses' home in Salford?'

'Not really.' Mary smiled, and eased herself a step or two further along the bank, holding on to trees to keep her balance. 'But let's not talk about failure. You said that Nepalese chap is paying in advance for his festival. That must surely mean we're well on course for our total. The arcade is already getting popular, as word gets round, and people tell other people about how good it is. It's doing great business, and the garden party raised thousands, not to mention the covenants that Paul charmed out of the pockets of the wealthy with his speech.'

'Ram Panjit's thousands certainly did the cause a lot of good. But Paul isn't speaking to me at the moment over that!' She smiled to herself. 'Not since he found out it was me who persuaded the rest of the committee that the festival was a good idea financially.'

'I thought that's how you liked it. Paul not speaking, I mean. You did say it caused you less aggravation?'

Robyn didn't reply. But the thought of going back to Chase Hey, with the enlightenment festival going ahead at the end of the month, knowing that Paul was still furious about the way she'd influenced the entire committee against his wishes, made her brave heart quail a little. She had been disturbed by his attentions at the time, but she missed them now. His indifference she thought she could cope with. But she wasn't at all sure about his fury! Even the thought that she was keeping her promise to Victoria by keeping him very much at arm's length didn't help to raise her spirits.

The sisters drove home, suntanned and relaxed, and Mary couldn't wait to get out into the garden. Amos Bridge was there, tying up chrysanthemums, and picking the first few ripe pears. He was a fresh-faced young man, who worked in his mother's smallholding most of the day, and spent his free time fulfilling his greatest love, that of showing others how to make things grow. 'Great to see you home. How about this marrow, Mary? Want to enter it in the local show?'

Robyn noticed that Amos greeted Mary with a kiss. They were perhaps better friends than Robyn realised, busy as she was for most of every week. Mary was laughing. 'Amos, it was you who insisted on growing it here. You enter it.' She paused. 'Better still, let's get money for the hospital! Give a prize to the one who guesses its weight!'

Robyn drove back to Chase Hey with apprehension. She had been grateful for the respite of life without the disturbing influence of Paul Howell-Jones. She knew inside herself that she couldn't wait to see him again. Yet however much she wanted him to be pleasant, and to be pleasant to him, she had to remember that he was buying a flat with Victoria. Buying a flat was a serious commitment. Robyn had to accept that, for all his persuasive words, his compliments and flattery towards her, Paul was concerned elsewhere, and not to be trusted. Anyway, he probably wasn't speaking!

The ward greeted her with a cheer. 'Florence Nightingale's here, folks. Give her a big hand. Sister West, you've been a long time away.'

Philomena Gorsey's bed was empty. Sally said, 'Paul thought it was time to see how she could cope by herself. She was quite agreeable to being discharged, when we told her she could come up and see you every time she came to Out-Patients.'

There was one bed where curtains had been drawn. Robyn looked at Sally for an explanation. 'Dr Howell-Jones had to come up to give Mrs Burns an injection for her piles.'

Robyn tried to ignore the lurch in her breast. Paul here at this hour? 'That's very nice of Dr Howell-Jones.'

Sally said with a smirk, 'He'll do anything for you, Sister. We could have asked the houseman, but the consultant said he would come himself. Nothing at all to do with the fact that his favourite sister was coming back this morning!'

'I see.' Robyn tried to sound tart.

'Don't you think you'd better go and assist?'

Robyn took a deep breath, and walked towards the curtains. Approaching a den with a man-eating tiger in it must feel something like this. Or did she mean a woman-eating tiger? Robyn slipped unobtrusively between the curtains. Paul was indeed busy, a large lady's naked flank hiding most of his top half. 'I'm sorry I wasn't here earlier, Mrs Burns. But you're in good hands now.'

The student nurse, who had been holding the tray of instruments, gave Robyn an agonised look. 'Can I go now, Sister?'

'Of course, Lyn. I'll take over here.' She took the little girl's place. Paul didn't even look. Robyn waved Lyn away, and settled herself at the consultant's side. She watched his rather rumpled collar, untidy brown curls, the green eyes above the white mask. There wasn't a man in the world who could matter to her as much as this one. But even on those rare occasions when he didn't argue with her, she knew now that his future would not be in Barnaby. He was buying a flat with Victoria. That was enough evidence for Robyn.

Paul sat up suddenly, withdrawing a syringe gently. 'How do you feel, Mrs Burns?'

'Didn't feel a thing, Doctor.'

'Good. Let Sister know if you're worried. But you should be fine now.'

'Thank you, Doctor.'

'Part of the service, Mrs Burns. Would you dress this, please, Sister?'

Robyn relieved him of the basin and syringe as they walked down the ward together. He kept his eyes fixed straight ahead. 'You can be so smarmy sometimes.'

'It's called a bedside manner, Sister West.'

'Don't forget you're in the north now, Dr Howell-Jones. We distrust people who are too nice.'

They reached the sanctity of her room. Paul said, 'Speak for yourself, Sister. Some ladies eat out of my hand.'

'Bully for them.'

His voice turned positively arctic. 'And some women haven't sold me down the river by sabotaging my entire committee to the Holy Enlightenment College.'

Here it comes. Still sore about the enlightenment festival, in spite of the boost to the funds, and the fortnight's holiday, during which she had hoped his anger would have cooled a little. Robyn said gently, 'Don't you think the end sometimes justifies the means? We're desperately in need of money. Ram Panjit wants to give us money—lots of it. Paul, you're a well-known consultant. You can work anywhere if Chase Hey closes. It means a hell of a lot more to the little people who work here. And the patients who need us. Can you imagine what it would do to Philomena's little life if she found the shutters up at Chase Hey? If I have to leave Meadow Cottage I don't know what Mary would do. I can't bear to think of it. But I feel for the patients even more.'

'Of course I feel for them too. And there are jobs around here for you. You could go on the district. I see your point, Robyn, but I think you're dramatising it a little. It wouldn't be the end of the world.' He was leaning on the door-frame, his arms folded, and his handsome face severe. 'And it is still my opinion that this silly festival will give the hospital a very bad name.'

Robyn looked away. 'Then you can arrange to be away in London that weekend. I'll make sure everyone knows that you didn't approve, and have nothing at all to do with it.'

'Don't tell me you mean to attend the damn thing?'

'Oh, yes. Someone has to make sure nothing goes wrong.'

'You're crazier than I thought, Robyn.' He picked up his stethoscope, and turned to go. She was just beginning to relax, grateful that his disapproval hadn't resulted in a blazing row, when he stopped and came back into the room. He was still very distant with her. 'By the way, you'll probably be glad to know that Swainson Black is home.'

'Paul, that's great news. Has he said anything about Chase Hey?'

'That's the point. Nothing. He's still very low. Not our fault, of course—it's a result of his injury. But it does mean his opinion of Chase Hey can't be too flattering at the moment, unfortunately. There's not much we can do about that, I'm afraid. But I think Mr Black might be our biggest problem. Even if we raise all the money, he could still refuse to allow the funding we need for staffing and equipment.'

'It seems very wrong for the decision to be in the hands of one man.'

'I know. I feel it might be politic to butter up a few other members of the health authority. Would it be appallingly forward of me to suggest that a little drinks party in your pretty garden might help to win friends and influence people?'

'At Meadow Cottage? You think so?'

'I'm sure of it.' His voice had lost its steel now, and the green eyes were warm with remembrance. 'When I remember the first time I ate with you——'

'You did invite yourself, as I recall.'

'I admit it. But I'll never forget the combination of a warm spring evening, you and your sister's genuine northern hospitality, the beauty of the garden—it's one of the happiest memories of my life, you know.'

'Is it really?' Robyn looked at him, wondering. Was he really the heel who tried to make love to one woman while being engaged to another? Perhaps, underneath, there was a nice man trying to get out. She knew that she wanted to believe in him. But after the garden party, and her promise to Victoria, she was reluctant to hope or believe too much. She added, 'You know Mary would love to give a party. Especially in a good cause.'

'Then will you do it? The action committee will pay for food and drink, of course. I thought maybe the weekend before your awful festival—to give the health authority people some good impressions of Chase Hey, not loony ones.'

Robyn smiled at that. 'You don't mince words, do you? But yes—I think it's a great idea. I'll do the inviting tonight. Mary can do the planning—she's good at that.'

'And she might even charm Swainson Black. She's quite persuasive, your little sister.'

'And I wonder if Philomena Gorsey would like to come along and help?' said Robyn very thoughtfully. 'If anyone can sing our praises it must be that little woman. It would be interesting to see Swainson Black chatting to Phil. . .'

The evening was indeed a golden one. The pear trees were heavy with mellow-smelling fruit, and the leaves were just turning crimson on the creepers. Rose-hips glowed in the hedges, and the late sun was warm on bare arms and floral dresses. Mary and Robyn handed round sparkling wine, fruit cup, cheese savouries and home-made cakes—and did their best to speak confidently of raising the money to keep Chase Hey viable.

It was almost midnight, and the sky was studded with stars, when the last of their visitors left. Robyn came back into the cottage after seeing them off, to find Paul Howell-Jones with his shirt-sleeves rolled up, busily washing the plates and glasses. 'Paul, there's no need——'

He turned and leaned on the sink, drying his hands. 'And who else would help you? Mary's gone to bed, and I've sent Philomena home. She was willing to stay, but she isn't strong enough for late nights yet.'

Robyn looked at him, touched by his thoughtfulness. But Mary? 'Bed?'

'Doctor's orders.'

'You mean you sent her to bed. Why? She always likes to stay up and see to the kitchen.'

Paul smiled, and Robyn felt a *frisson* of apprehension at the way he was looking at her. He said in a low voice, 'I think you know why, Bobbie.'

Memories of being in his arms, of her helplessness at the passion of his kisses, and her eager response last time, made Robyn ruthless. 'Please go. Now! Don't argue with me, Paul. I don't want to raise my voice. But go.'

His eyes were half closed, sensuous and misty. He murmured, moving fractionally closer to her in the little flagged kitchen, 'I'm not one of your nurses, Bobbie. You can't speak to me like that.'

'I can and I will.' She put her hands on her hips. 'You can't be much of a gentleman, to stay when I don't want you.'

'You do want me, though.' He didn't touch her, but she was held by the mesmerism in his eyes, and stood rooted to the spot, unable to look away, and unable to deny that he spoke the truth. He went on, his husky voice almost a whisper, 'I asked you to do this party for the sake of the hospital, Bobbie. But I admit that I was desperately homesick to be invited here again. Why have you kept me away?'

'You know very well why. I was embarrassed and hurt by the way Victoria caught us together at the garden party. She blamed me for trying to trap you. It isn't going to happen again. I've no intention of trying to trap you. I don't want to see you ever again, except on a professional basis. Is that clear enough for you?' Her voice rose, in spite of her good intentions, as Paul remained totally unmoved by her words, and even edged another inch towards her, his lips curled in a teasing smile.

'But I'm lonely, Bobbie.'

'My heart bleeds,' she said savagely. 'Try and hold on for another week, Paul. You're going back to Victoria Alexander on Saturday, aren't you, to escape the festival? She'll help you forget your loneliness.'

Paul stood up straighter then. 'Why go on about Vicki? She's only a friend, you know. I believe it's my sports car she's in love with if anything. I didn't invite her to the garden party, you know. I swear I didn't.'

'Just made sure she knew when it was!'

He ran his fingers through his brown curls, unruly now after his head had been over the washing-up. He looked tired suddenly, and vulnerable. With an impatient gesture, he turned and walked through to the living-room, and sat on the sofa, smoothing his hair back again. Robyn watched him from the doorway. After a while he looked up at her. 'I was born in a cottage like this.'

'In Wales?' Robyn softened her voice now, unable to keep up her opposition to a man she cared for so much. 'Do you still go back?'

'No.' There was a silence. Robyn crept further into the room, and sat on the arm of the sofa. Paul didn't seem to notice. He went on, 'I never appreciated it till it was too late. I suppose I kept quiet about my humble background because all my friends at medical school came from wealthier homes. I used to visit them, but never invite them back. And suddenly it was too late; Dad died and Mother went to live in a home.'

'I'm sorry.'

'I deserved it. But they didn't. They scrimped for

years for my education, and I repaid them in money, but not in love.'

Robyn said softly, encouragingly, 'It isn't easy for a junior doctor to get much time off. Especially when you were studying as well. I'm sure they knew that.'

He looked up at her and shook his head. 'I would have found the time if I'd really wanted. You know that. If I had my time over again, I'd make sure I found the time. Success isn't everything.'

'I'm sure they were terrifically proud of you.'

He sighed again. 'Maybe.'

She said quietly, 'Well, perhaps I was hard, telling you not to visit here. Come when you like, Paul—but don't send Mary to bed again, and don't expect anything from me except friendship.'

He smiled then. 'Thanks, Bobbie. You're a great girl really, and I ought never to argue with you. Well, I'd better be off, I suppose. I'm keeping you up.'

'You are. I've had a busy day.'

'I'm sorry.' He stood up quickly, and went to the front door. She followed him as he opened it, letting in the stars, and the sweet scent of thyme, mint and lavender. 'Oh, my jacket.'

'I'll get it.' She brought his jacket from where he had left it over a chairback, and he slung it over his shoulder. Tonight she saw him differently. In spite of the expensive clothes, the gold cuff-links and the scarlet sports car, she saw a lonely man, someone who had reached his goal in life, and yet found it filled with emptiness. 'Goodnight, Paul.'

Her face was tilted to his. He bent and touched her cheek with his lips. Then he kissed her lips. It was without aggression or passion this time. But it was incredibly sweet, and she found herself returning the

kiss with equal gentle hunger. When at last he drew
away, he reached out and caressed her cheek with his
hand, and the touch was dynamite. If at that moment
he had wanted to stay. . .'Goodnight, Bobbie,' he
whispered.

In the ward on Monday, Robyn noticed that their
relationship was suddenly easier. Though he still grimaced at any mention of the enlightenment festival, he
was somehow gentler with her, closer, more genuine.
She wondered if perhaps he had told no one else about
his parents, that maybe that moment of frankness had
turned them from acquaintances and colleagues into
real friends.

The organisers of the enlightenment festival were
mainly young British people, once the sort called
hippy, who either wore their hair very long and
unkempt, or had their heads shaved. They wore long
robes that left one shoulder bare, and called everyone
Brother or Sister. They seemed very peaceful and
polite as they arrived on the Friday to erect tents and
draperies, and to build a little stage with an altar in
the middle.

Paul was less scathing that day, as he finished his
clinic, and came up to the ward to do a quick ward-
round before the weekend. 'They seem the harmless
enough type of loonies,' he commented. 'I suppose a
couple of days of chanting and meditation won't do
the hospital any lasting harm.'

'And will do our bank account a lot of good,'
reminded Robyn.

He grinned and nodded. 'Well, enjoy yourself. See
you on Monday.' He handed her the patients' notes,
and signed the drug prescriptions. 'Tony knows what

to do about Mrs Burns. And the diabetics will keep their own charts, OK? Just check that nobody forgets.'

She watched him go, striding down the corridor. Then she went to the window, to watch him emerge from the front door and go to his Lotus and sling an overnight bag into the back.She wondered what sort of house Victoria and Paul lived in. Maybe modest, maybe grand. But somehow she knew it couldn't be as special as Meadow Cottage, though he seemed pleased enough to be going to London. Robyn leaned her elbows on the window ledge to get a better view.

Suddenly Paul stuck his head out of the window, looked directly up at Robyn, and, grinning broadly at her obvious interest, he blew her a kiss. Blushing, she gave him a little embarrassed wave, and turned away quickly from the window as the Lotus roared out of the hospital drive into the busy country road that led him away from Barnaby.

After work Robyn joined some of the arcade pro-prietors, who had closed their shops early and were standing in the grounds watching the strange sect, who had finished putting up their tents, and now sat on the ground cross-legged, their eyes closed and their fingers crooked upwards. They were murmuring a repetitive chant, over and over again. Jackie Darcy looked fascinated, while some of the nurses and porters were openly amused.

Robyn noticed a police car turn into the hospital drive. There didn't appear to be anyone else from the campaign committee around, so she went across and greeted the driver, and asked him whom he wanted to speak to.

'It's Sister West, isn't it? You looked after Mam when she had her heart trouble.' The constable was a burly, soft-spoken man from the next road to Meadow Cottage. 'Tell you the truth, Sister, I've been advised that some of these people use drugs. I'm afraid I've got a warrant to search all the tents. I don't want to cause alarm. I've got a sniffer dog in the back. Mind if I let him out?'

'Of course not. I'll walk with you, to make it look less official, shall I?'

Drugs. Why hadn't she thought of that? Robyn walked at the constable's side. But the dog had already scampered into a marquee, and emerged dragging a woven bag which he laid on the grass and then barked excitedly.

The constable knelt and looked inside the bag. He tipped out a small plastic bag, opened a corner, and tipped out some of the contents. He sniffed at them, and then he tasted a minute sample on the tip of his finger. He looked up at an anxious Robyn. 'I'm sorry, Sister. It's cannabis. This is serious. We can't allow any festival to go on now. There's no knowing how much of this there'll be about. It's against the law, Sister. Sorry.'

Her spirits sank, but Robyn was not one to let events get her down. She knew the officer was only fulfilling instructions. 'That's all right. Don't apologise. We can't have anything like a scandal here. It's a blessing you found it before the rest of the "followers" arrived.'

'It's going to be a big job, turning everyone away before they get here. We'll need several cars to block off the motorways. Still, I bet you're relieved that the name of the hospital will be in the clear. It wouldn't do the reputation of Chase Hey much good if this news got out.'

Robyn felt her cheeks growing warm. The reputation of Chase Hey. . . And everyone on the committee knew that Robyn West had been the driving force in allowing this festival to go ahead. Had she, single-handedly, out of sheer sexual jealousy and pique, brought the entire campaign to an ignominious conclusion? 'Do you think—the news will get out?'

The young constable stopped in his examination of the evidence, and from his face she knew he appreciated her predicament. 'The *Recorder* won't get anything from me, Sister West, I promise you.'

'Thank you. Thank you very much.' She stopped herself from telling him how valuable their reputation was to them at that moment in the year. He seemed to understand.

And then just the voice she didn't want to hear. Ross Cartwright, hands in pockets, baggy sweater and rumpled ginger hair, stopped at her side. 'Are you having some sort of problem, Robyn?'

'Nothing I can't handle, Ross, thanks.' And at that moment a waif-like figure emerged from the tent from where the cannabis had been dragged. It was Philomena Gorsey. Her eyes were glassy, and there was an inane smile on her lips, in spite of the worried frown and the deathly-pale cheeks. 'Phil!'

The girl-woman turned to Robyn and her smile broadened. 'You're home, Sister! Can I stay in Chase Hey with you now?'

'Oh, Phil.' Her poor little problem patient. But Robyn held out her arms, and Philomena's frown faded as she nestled against Robyn's chest.

CHAPTER SEVEN
October

THE campaign committee sat round Tom Gordon's mahogany table in the administrator's room, and looked very glum indeed. After a while, Robyn said, 'It's very nice of you not to say, "I told you so". I have to take full responsibility for the fiasco of the festival. I ought to have made sure they kept to the rules. I do realise that the affair might have ruined everything.'

Tom Gordon said kindly, 'You weren't to know about their habits, Robyn. An innocent girl like you.'

John Crabtree said, 'Well, at least we're not implicated. The police were pretty good about it, really. I'm just disappointed that poor Philomena got caught up in it all. Sometimes I think she's more of a fixture at Chase Hey than you, Tom.'

Robyn had been trying not to look at Paul Howell-Jones at the head of the table. She said, 'Just because she was hanging about watching—just as we all were. She is so attached to this place. Now she's got her wish and is back in my ward yet again.'

Paul took a breath to speak, and Robyn didn't look at him. But he said, not looking at her either, in a surprisingly normal voice, 'So we'll just say no more about it. But I'd like to point out my own opposition all along. Maybe the committee would like to take more notice of me next time?'

Robyn was suddenly incensed. 'I've apologised for the mess I got us into. And I apologise too for the loss of the three thousand pounds we were expecting from Ram Panjit. But I don't apologise for trying to raise money to save this hospital, Dr Howell-Jones, and I don't think it necessary to take that tone with me. I wasn't the only member of this committee who thought that.' So much for their new-found friendship. This meeting had made sure that their relationship was back to the low it had achieved after their very first committee meeting—that of distant coolness on Robyn's part, and self-righteous arrogance on his.

John intercepted in his gruff Lancashire voice, 'I think we ought to be deciding on a fund-raising function for this month. No use looking back. It's over, and thank goodness it didn't get into the papers. Mr Cartwright was very good about it. Now, what do members think of a Hallowe'en party? Fancy dress, with generous prizes, should bring in the townsfolk.'

Paul nodded. 'All in favour? Good idea, John—but somehow I can't see us reaching that target now. You're right, Robyn—I didn't like the idea of holy enlightenment—but I admit I was counting on its money. We'll have to go all out—maybe get more people from the town involved.'

Robyn suggested, 'Why not coopt Ross Cartwright on to this committee? He's done a lot for us already. Maybe he'd be willing for the *Recorder* to donate one of the prizes?'

Paul gave her a look of grudging praise. She recalled that it was Paul who had pointed out Ross's admiration for her. But he was detached. 'Good thinking. I wonder if some of the local businesses might be approached too? They'd get the publicity, and we'd get better prizes.'

The discussion continued, as decisions were taken

to hold the party in the arcade, and to ask the ladies who ran the whole-food café to do the catering. Someone said, 'And I'm sure Sister West would have some spare apples to bob for. I propose we forget about sticky buns—too messy.'

It was getting dark when the meeting drew to a close. 'Thank you all,' said Paul. 'It can't be helped, but that three thousand would have come in very handy. And there's still the matter of Councillor Swainson Black. Sister West's evening party was a success as far as the rest of the health authority were concerned, but Black is still obviously not on our side. I'm afraid we need some more suggestions, ladies and gentlemen. Come and see me any time, if you get a brainwave.'

As they made their way to the entrance hall Robyn caught up with Paul. 'Who's looking after Councillor Black?'

'He was in the surgical ward. Under Claude Sarmsworth. Why?'

'Is he attending OPD?'

'Don't know. I could ask Sarmsworth.'

He was still waiting for an explanation. Robyn shuffled her feet. 'It's just that—well—I believe Mary has something. . .that might help his depression.'

There was a pause. The night porter switched on the lights in the lobby—which didn't brighten things much, as they were economising by using low-wattage bulbs. Paul said quietly, 'Herbalism, Robyn?'

'Herbalism, holistic medicine, self-healing, folk-medicine, witchcraft, black magic—call it what you like!' Robyn blazed at him suddenly. 'For God's sake, you ask for suggestions, and when I offer you a perfectly good one you sneer like a—a—typical London yuppie.'

'Oops—lovers' tiff!' Two junior nurses passed by, and Robyn heard their comments with a blush. Lovers, indeed. She had drawn closer to Paul in the first half of the year. But now they seemed as far apart as ever.

Paul said, 'I'll ask Sarmsworth if Black is attending Out-Patients. Will that suit you?'

'Yes.'

'Don't sulk, Robyn. You'll get frown-lines.'

She looked up, furious with him. But Paul was teasing her, and his expression was gentle. She said more calmly, 'If Mr Sarmsworth would transfer him to your clinic would you be willing to bring him in for a few days? Would you think it ethical enough to try something that Mary makes?'

'Not really. What clinical trials have you done? What results have you got that a placebo wouldn't? I like to have my therapy properly tested before I give it to a patient. Can you prove anything at all, except superstition?'

'I don't know. But I'll try and get you some evidence, OK? I'll have a word with Jackie—she should have something for you. She's read a lot. We have so little time left for anything to work.'

'True. All right. Give me some proof, and I'll get our friend the councillor in for some tests.'

'Thanks, Paul.' She had won a minor victory! She said, trying not to sound pleased, 'I know how much you'd hate to be proved wrong. But I'm afraid it has to be done.' And, with a little wave of the hand, she ran out into the car park.

Someone was coming towards her. At first she thought in the dusk that it was a woman, but then she realised that it was Mr Ram Panjit in his white turban and robes. 'Sister West?'

'Hello, Mr Panjit.' Her voice was cold. 'The police let you go, then?'

'I am not implicated, Sister West. Some of my followers are like children. I must reprimand them. I do not take drugs myself, no alcohol, tobacco, not even tea and coffee. They are not following me closely enough. They must pay their own fines. And you must believe me when I tell you I had no knowledge whatever of that poor village girl you found.'

She nodded, wearily. She did believe him. He was too nice to lie. 'I'm sorry it ended the way it did. But it's over now.'

'I wanted to apologise to your committee. They were very kind to me, and I appreciate it. Here is a contribution to your funds. I pray you do not have to close your pleasant hospital. I'd be grateful if you would hand this to your treasurer. Goodnight, Sister West.'

She stood with a white envelope in her hand, too stunned to say anything. 'Thank you very much,' she echoed to Mr Panjit's retreating back. 'It's very kind. . .'

Then she rushed inside again. 'Where's Dr Howell-Jones?' But the familiar roar of his powerful engine showed that she had missed him by seconds. She put the envelope in her bag, and drove home thoughtfully. It probably wouldn't be much. But it was better than nothing.

'Why don't you open it?' Mary was as curious as her sister.

'After dinner.'

'Why not now?'

'It won't be worth anything. I don't want to be disappointed.'

'Oh, come on, Bobbie—open it!'

It was a cheque for two thousand pounds. The girls stared at it. 'Two thousand? For nothing! How marvellous. What a gentleman.'

'I must get hold of Paul tonight.' But she didn't know where he would be. She could try the hospital residence. He may have just gone out to a local pub for dinner. She rang the residence, but there was no reply from Paul's flat.

Jackie Darcy rang the bell. 'Just brought Mary my shopping-list for next week.'

'Come in, Jackie.'

'Thought we could go along to the Three Bells for a drink, girls.'

'I've got some phoning to do. You go, Mary. Explain that Paul needs some hard evidence before he'll try your prescription for Councillor Black's depression.' After the other two had gone, Robyn rang again.

The telephonist laughed. 'You and Dr Howell-Jones seem to see a lot of one another. He was asking where you were just ten minutes ago! But he's gone out again now. Watch it, Robyn—people are beginning to talk.'

Robyn put the phone down slowly. People were talking. Silly people, when there was nothing whatever to gossip about. . . She sat at the table, pushing her used plates to one side, and put her chin on her hands, staring into space. Even if she did love Paul, he didn't love her, not in the same way—and, anyway, she had made a promise to Victoria. She was better not thinking of him. Yet she couldn't help it. How much could promises mean, when human emotions were concerned?

'The door was open.' A deep voice. A familiar voice, one that she heard continually in her heart.

'Paul!' She looked up with unaffected pleasure. 'Jackie mustn't have shut it properly.'

'I hear you've been looking for me.' He sat opposite her, brushed some crumbs on the table to make a space for his elbows, and looked at her hard. 'So I came over. What were you thinking about?'

'Nothing.'

'Tell me the truth.'

'No.'

'Such insubordination! Why did you ring me, then?' Robyn smiled slightly, and pushed the cheque across the tablecloth towards him. 'Ram Panjit?' He smiled broadly as he unfolded the cheque, and realised how much was there. 'I see. You felt guilty at losing the money. This must make you feel much better. He's a generous man—he can afford to be, I believe.'

'Doesn't it make you feel better too?'

'Frankly, yes, it does. Well done, Robyn.'

'I didn't do anything.'

'It must have been those big brown eyes that charmed him.' Robyn looked away suddenly. Paul folded the cheque and put it in his wallet. 'I just had a bite at the Three Bells with Ross Cartwright. He's willing to donate a prize for the Hallowe'en do—and give it generous coverage. Isn't it time that you and he came to some understanding? He's dotty about you in his own quiet way.'

'Then it's funny he never comes round to tell me so. You come visiting more than he does.'

'Is that so?' His eyes were very green in the light

the table-lamp. Robyn realised that they'd been talking quickly, flippantly, as though they were both trying to hide something. Paul said, 'He would come if you gave him more encouragement.'

'What is it to you if I'm an old maid, Paul? I like my life, you know. Why interfere?'

'I don't like to see you looking so lonely and thoughtful. You have such a nice smile, you know. You should be happy more often.'

She couldn't help smiling then. 'It's the people I work with, Doctor—especially my boss. He's so wrong about so many things that we seldom—if ever—agree about anything.'

'You wicked woman!' Laughing, he came round to her side of the table, and caught her tightly in his arms. 'You should have a good hiding, you know. Such disloyalty to the man you ought to be supporting. Most nurses think I'm Superman.'

Struggling in his grip, laughing with frustration at his superior strength, Robyn said, 'Why don't you fly away, then?'

He let her go suddenly, and stood facing her with his arms at his sides. 'I'm sorry. I know I make myself too much at home in your house. You didn't ask me to stay, and I shouldn't have been so pushy.'

She looked up into his beloved face, and said gently, 'But Paul, dear, you always were pushy. It's the way you're made.'

For a moment he didn't reply. Then he took her in arms, and held her close for a moment before her. This time he didn't stop after one kiss, but move his hands over her body with infinite every touch making her need for him he kissed her cheek, her jaw and down to her neck and shoulder, Robyn murmured, 'I didn't mean to say that. I'm sorry, truly I am.'

'Doesn't matter. It's true. Kiss me, Bobbie.'

'But——'

'It's the only way to stop you arguing with me,' he explained throatily, holding her head in both hands and kissing her mouth again with expert lips and tongue. Robyn gave up any thoughts of promises to Victoria, and resentment at his taking possession of her mind and her body without even a by-your-leave. This was the only man who had ever stirred her to these heights of pleasure, and she was reluctant for it to come to an end. Besides, what was the harm? He would only be here for a few more months.

The sound of the key in the lock made them both draw apart with flushed faces. Robyn tossed back her hair, and pulled her sweater back from her shoulder to its proper place. She sat swiftly at the table again, while Paul sat casually on the sofa, and picked up the latest edition of the *Recorder*. Jackie wheeled Mary into the living-room, before going back to shut the door. 'Right, my lady. Tea, coffee or cocoa?' Then she looked into the room, where Robyn greeted them with a feeble grin. 'I say, I didn't realise——'

Paul said with a grin, 'I didn't know you drank coffee, Jackie. That's not a good advertisement for your trade, is it? All that caffeine?'

The joke took away any possible embarrassment, and Robyn went to the kitchen to take the dinner-tray away, and put the kettle on, leaving Paul and Jackie discussing the merits of coffee as opposed to camomile tea as an evening drink. Mary followed Robyn into the kitchen. 'Sorry to barge in.'

'No problem. He only called for the cheque.'

'Yes, I see.' Mary got out the best china mugs, tactfully saying nothing more. 'Shall we have tea? Jackie doesn't mind.'

'I think Paul would prefer tea too.'

'Ross Cartwright was in the pub.'

'I know. Paul had dinner with him. Why didn't you ask him back?'

'For one thing I didn't realise Paul would be here. And for another—he seemed preoccupied. Not as friendly as usual.'

Robyn said nothing, but her heart wept for Mary, who deserved someone nice, and who would make Ross a good wife. Why couldn't he like Mary instead of Robyn? 'He's probably quite busy. The Chase Hey campaign has been going strong for six months now. On top of his ordinary work, that's quite a lot of overtime.'

'Quite busy? More like quite drunk, I'd say.'

'Oh, dear.'

'Have your hurt your neck?'

Robyn covered the red mark made by Paul's impatient lips with her fingers, and didn't reply. She hoped it would have gone by the time she went back to work in the morning. It was one thing to be swept away in a tide of passion, but quite another for it to show.

It proved to be good occupational therapy to get her patients interested in making black cut-outs of witches to decorate the ward. 'And, while we have a fund-raising party in the arcade, you can have your own party up here, as long as you don't make much noise. It is a hospital, after all.'

'It's the best hospital in the country,' asserted Mrs

Burns. 'It's just too bad that I'll be going home and I'll miss Hallowe'en in here.'

'I'm sure you'd rather be in your own home, with all the ghoulies and bogies around,' laughed Robyn, handing out scissors. 'Chase Hey might just be a bit wild on Hallowe'en!'

Philomena was looking bright. She had only taken the one smoke of cannabis, and showed no sign of wanting to try it again. 'Are you going with Dr Howell-Jones, Sister?'

Robyn realised that the gossip was still going strong, and did her best to defuse it. 'All members of the campaign group will have to be there. Dr Howell-Jones is the chairman.'

'What are you wearing, Sister?' Philomena persisted.

'Something quite horrible, with warts and green teeth,' she teased. 'I might give you a preview!'

On the night of the party the arcade people had outdone themselves, with trailing 'cobwebs' and netting holding ugly little owls, tarantulas and bats, and other cardboard nasties with many pairs of legs and waving phosphorescent antennae.

Robyn hurried home, where Mary had two rucksacks of best Cox's apples, and a basketful of homemade buns. But it was her hair that startled Robyn. 'Mary! What have you done to it? Is it a wig?'

Mary giggled. 'No, it's my own. I got the girl in the hairdressers to do it—very strong gel. Do I look like a werewolf?'

'You look like an android,' moaned Robyn, gazing with disappointment at Mary's hair, which stood on end in a series of spikes. 'Your beautiful curls.'

'Well, I'm a spook, and spooks are supposed to look

horrid,' grinned her sister. 'Now, all I need is my sheet, and I'm ready. Hurry up, Bobbie. We need time to put the apples in water.' And while Robyn tried to overcome her tiredness and dress up in a short black shirt, black stockings with holes in them, stiletto heels, and one of Jackie's voluminous capes with a pointed hood, Mary went on, 'I hope you don't mind, Sis, but I've invited Amos. He's been so kind, helping with the apples.'

'Of course not. But I hope he knows you're going to look disgusting!'

As Robyn drove the three of them, Amos dressed as Dracula, and having trouble keeping his teeth in place, she fervently hoped they wouldn't have a puncture and have to get out. But they arrived safely, and were greeted at the door by taped weeping and wailing, and the tall figure of Paul dressed as Merlin. 'Well, he was a Welshman too,' he said, steadying his tall hat and the stuffed owl sewn on to his shoulder.

'How are the tickets going?'

'Very well. I think we could have charged more than five pounds. Never mind. Maybe they'll buy lots of refreshments.' He looked Robyn up and down. 'You look quite wicked, Bobbie, but how the devil are you going to dance in those shoes?'

She put her hand to her forehead, feeling suddenly faint. 'I think I'm too tired to dance anyway.'

'You've been overdoing it.' His expression was concerned, his voice suddenly urgent. He took her gently over to a seat. 'And Mary says you haven't been eating properly. Better get you some vitamins and iron tomorrow. I thought you had more sense than to neglect your own health.'

She smiled at him in the darkness. If only he realised

why she had been off her food. He left her, to greet
more arrivals at the door, but Paul kept coming back
every so often to make sure she was all right. On one
of these occasions he had put his arm round her
shoulders, and was teasing her that she should come
to work in that miniskirt. They were both laughing,
their heads close together, when there was a flash, and
they realised their photograph had been taken. 'Ready
for you at the end of the evening, Paul! A tenner for
the negative!' It was Ross Cartwright. And he wasn't
laughing.

It was after midnight, and the prizes had been
awarded. Paul took Robyn in his arms for the last
dance, neither of them even thinking of looking for
anyone else. 'You look all in. Look, why don't I drive
you home, and Amos can drive your car?'

She nodded, almost asleep on her feet. 'It's been a
long day.'

'Where is Amos?'

They looked around in the dimness. 'My God, he's
dancing. With Mary!' And there, on her feet, with
Amos's strong arms supporting her, Mary was swaying
from side to side, a blissful expression on her face.
There was another flash, and Ross had caught the
moment too.

Tired, but elated suddenly at the sight of her sister
actually dancing, unselfconsciously close to Amos,
Robyn followed Paul, who pulled off his sorcerer's
robe, to reveal jeans and a T-shirt underneath. She
said, 'It's kind of you. I can manage, you know.'

'No, I'm worried about you. I want to see you safe.'

'Thanks, Paul. You're nice. Sometimes I wonder
why I'm so rude to you.'

'Because I'm a pain in the butt, probably. Now you

sit just here, while I bring the car to the door. Won't be a jiffy.'

She sat obediently in the hall. The dancing was still going on, and strains of smoochy music filtered out into the low-watt shadows. She was weary, but suddenly aware that someone else sat in the hall a few chairs away. 'Why, Ross. What are you doing out here?'

'Keeping an eye on you. I don't like the way he's been monopolising you all night. He's got a girlfriend, you know.'

'He's only being kind.' But her excuse sounded weak.

The Lotus drew up at the door, and Paul ran lightly up the steps to help Robyn down. Ross's face was black. He stood up and said, 'Robyn's all-in, man. Why can't you leave her alone? Can't you see that she doesn't want you and your poncey car and your London ways?'

'Hey, steady on. I thought we'd buried the hatchet.' Paul was wary, his voice quiet and reasonable.

'I've nothing against you as a doctor—or a campaign manager. But you sure as hell don't know how to treat a lady. Can't you see what you've done to her? Before you came to Barnaby she was a strong, rosy young woman. Everyone knew Robyn West, and she had the time and energy to stop off and chat with her neighbours. Always cheerful, she was. Everyone's noticed the way she's gone—all peaky and thin and pale.'

Paul drew himself up. 'It's nearly winter, Ross. No one has a suntan in winter, OK?'

'Don't patronise me, Jones. I've had quite enough of this. I'm warning you now, I'm not standing aside and letting you do this to Robyn. She means too much to me.'

'She means a lot to me too, so just lay off, man, and don't make a fool of yourself. You've had too much to drink. I'm taking her home, so get out of the way, please?'

It happened very quickly, but Robyn shrank back in horror as Ross Cartwright lashed out at Paul with a clenched fist. Paul ducked, and the blow missed. Ross lost his balance, and spread-eagled himself on the hospital lobby linoleum with a sickening thud.

CHAPTER EIGHT
November

MIST hung on the hedgerows, on the bare trees, and made the cobwebs sparkle on the ivy over the grey walls of Meadow Cottage. Robyn had missed the Bonfire Night fireworks, confined to bed by flu and exhaustion. But she knew it was more than that. Ross Cartwright's fierce condemnation of Paul had upset them both, and it was a relief in a way that Robyn was cared for by her own GP, and that Paul thought it wiser not to visit her for a little while.

'My blood tests are back to normal,' complained Robyn when Mary brought her supper. 'Why am I so weak?'

'Do you really want my personal diagnosis?' said Mary. 'I can guess what's really wrong, though I expect you'll deny it. You always do.'

Robyn didn't deny anything. She felt too wretched. 'I'll get over it. It's when—things turn nasty. I'll never understand why Ross Cartwright was so boorish to Paul. There was just no need for it.' She sipped her soup, and laid`the spoon down again. 'And if Ross thought it would make me like him more the effect was just the opposite. I had no idea his feelings were so strong.'

'I did,' said Mary quietly.

Robyn looked at her sister, envying her the air of tranquillity that seemed to come from inside, making her face beautiful. 'I wonder how you always manage to look calm and controlled, Mary? You have so much more than most people have to put up with, but you never seem sorry for yourself. Yet here am I—with a touch of flu, feeling like death!'

Mary smiled. 'You've never asked me that before. I suppose you were too busy getting on with your job. But yes, I used to feel sorry for myself—especially about not dancing any more. It took a lot of thinking, and a lot of reading. And of course, when I met Jackie, she helped me a lot. I know people think she's eccentric—but she taught me how to think myself well.'

'Think myself well.' Robyn repeated the words obediently, but she didn't believe them. She had always believed in Mary's talent for healing, but now that it was her own feelings that were wounded, her own heart hurting, she was as sceptical as Paul Howell-Jones ever was of the superstitious side to meditation and self-help. 'I'll do my best. But how do I start?'

'You really want to know?'

'Yes, Mary, I really do.'

Mary poked at the log fire, making flickering shadows on the walls. Her voice was very low and musical just then. 'It's all about the way you see yourself, Bobbie. If you see yourself as a victim——'

'Oh, but I don't!' Robyn's retort was too quick, and she apologised. 'I think maybe I do. Somehow I think of young Philomena when you say that. She's weak and pathetic, and people like Sally say she ought to try and pull herself together. And now I'm the same—but it's worse, because I know I'm just a victim of my own foolish feelings, and I ought to be able to control them. Victim of Victoria Alexander, who is so much more beautiful and successful than I'll ever be.'

Mary nodded. 'You have to believe yourself beautiful. Truly believe it. Beautiful and healthy. Think of yourself in a lovely calm place—I always think of my garden in the middle of summer.'

'I can do that.'

'Can you feel it, Bobbie? The warmth of the sun, the feeling of being pretty and fit and strong—capable of anything?'

Robyn said gently, 'You can honestly feel that?'

Mary smiled. 'It took some practice,' she admitted. 'But it's easy now.'

Robyn leaned back against the cushions and closed her eyes. 'So—I'm being bathed by a mellow warm sun, under the pear trees, with the smell of the roses and the honeysuckle all around me. I know I'm a beautiful woman, with a demanding job, which I do better than anyone else——' She burst out laughing. 'It's no use. I can't. It seems so—big-headed, to believe things like that.'

Her sister smiled, because Robyn hadn't laughed like that for a long time. 'It's about self-esteem. You have to try. It isn't being big-headed—just quietly confident of your own worth, and your own place in the world.' Mary took the soup bowl, and wheeled herself to the kitchen with it. 'I'll leave you alone for a while. It's easier when no one's watching.'

Robyn heard her rattling cups and cutlery. Then Mary went through to her own room, and Robyn heard her making some phone calls. Lucky Mary, to have such self-control, to have made her own life so fulfilled and content. Robyn had always thought of herself as the strong one. She knew now that Mary could cope so much better with life, having had to face up to her problems of ill-health so early, to face them

and overcome them. Even over Ross Cartwright. . .
Mary had known he loved Robyn, not herself. Robyn
picked up the book that Mary had left at her bedside.
It was entitled *Healing, my story of Self-Help* and it
was written by Jackie Darcy.

It was late when Robyn finished the book. Jackie,
as well as Mary, had come to natural medicine because
of her own personal weakness. It was difficult to see
the bold, confident Jackie as the victim of a nervous
breakdown, of lack of self-assurance, and agorapho-
bia, confined to her home because she was afraid to go
out, terrified of meeting people, and going into acute
panic attacks at the very thought of taking a bus or a
train. . .Yet that was Jackie's story.

Robyn slept well that night, and woke refreshed.
One phrase from Jackie's book had stayed with her
through the night—something about healing being the
intuitive skill of working with nature. It made such
sense. Robyn washed and dressed, and went into the
kitchen with a new glow of hope. Jackie and Mary had
changed their own lives, and were spending them now
helping others find the same inner peace. November
might be drab and chill outside. She wondered how
long this glow would stay with her, once she returned
to the worries and strains of life at the doomed Chase
Hey hospital. Surely Paul must have a heart of stone,
to treat the philosophy of these gentle, loving, sincere
people with scornful indifference, however fond of
them he was growing on a personal level. 'The intuitive
skill of working with nature. . .'

Paul Howell-Jones was doing his ward-round in his
usual brisk, capable manner. 'Glad you're over your
flu, Robyn. You must be careful of your diet, you
know. Eat more—and better.' He handed her the

patient's file and moved on to the next bed. 'Have we an X-ray for this lady?'

Robyn moved round with him. But she noticed now that when Paul prescribed tablets or medicines the patients were less animated than when he spent a few moments of his time speaking to them by name, examining them carefully, expressing a few words of sympathy and understanding. Jackie was right. All this personal touching, the gentleness of his skilled hands, was part of the healing process, not just the pills.

'And Philomena? Shall we let you go home?' Home was a room in a council flat not being used by a distant and unloving cousin. Robyn wasn't surprised when Philomena's face clouded over. Paul hesitated. 'I'll have a chat with Sister. OK?'

Back in the office, Robyn said, 'Give her another few days, Paul. I've got a feeling I know something that might help. You don't need the bed, do you?'

'Not at the moment. Here's the admission list up to date.' Robyn looked down at the paper, and Paul said suddenly, 'What are you looking so smug about, Robyn?'

She was going through the list of admissions, and she looked up with a smile. 'Councillor Black! You're having him in.'

'Yes—as you requested. He does seem low. I hope we can find something to account for it in the tests.'

'Will you do one thing for me?'

'What's that? I don't promise.'

'Go down to the arcade when you've a moment, and have a word with Jackie Darcy?'

'The mad woman in the cape? Certainly not. I've a reputation to consider.'

'Paul—you told me you would try alternative treatment if I could prove it worked. Well—I think Jackie could prove it. She has some literature which I believe every medical person should read.' She looked vainly into his face for any sign of softening. 'Especially before you start treating Mr Black. And Philomena.'

Paul smiled briefly. 'Phil I'll leave to you, because you know her inside out. Medically she's fit. But Black—well, I know you mean well, my dear, and I've gone so far as to bring him in at your request. But I am the doctor, with an extensive list of qualifications and experience behind me. Don't try to teach me medicine, please, Robyn? I've treated post-traumatic reactive depression before with success. I'll stick to the medicine, if you'll stick to nursing, OK?'

'Yes, Doctor.'

'Hey—don't look so disappointed. I know my job. I don't have to take any notice of a bunch of cranks. You know I've included relaxation on your recommendation. But that's it, Robyn. I don't include witchcraft and black magic in my therapeutics, and that's flat.'

'It isn't black magic, Paul—it's tender magic.' He paused on his way out, and looked at her hard. Taking advantage of his interest, she went on, 'Don't you think someone like Mary knows a thing or two about depression? About the failure of conventional medicine?'

'Mary? She's the sunniest creature I've ever met.'

'Exactly.' Robyn turned back to her desk, knowing that to push her point now would be to lose it. 'And do you know why? Think it over, Paul.'

It was raining when she went off duty—that hard, constant rain that drummed on the shining wet grey slates of the roof, and made the windows impossible to see out of. Robyn shivered as she left the hospital

building to go to her car. She could see the lights of
the arcade, where the shops were still open, and hear
some hammering, where yet another shop space was
being prepared for a new client. A new rent-payer!
Robyn smiled to herself. Surely the campaign funds
had a chance now of hitting their target. Everything
they had planned had brought in money, and the
investment account was bringing in a good rate of
interest.

She drove home, windscreen wipers at full speed
against the driving sleet. There would be snow on the
Pennines if this went on. Meadow Cottage was in
darkness. Mary must be with Jackie, or maybe at the
pharmacy where the distillations of her plants were
prepared. Robyn put the kettle on, and lit the fire,
brightening the shadows with a red glow. On the
mantelpiece was a note from Mary saying she wouldn't
be home for supper.

The telephone rang. It was John Crabtree's wife,
inviting Robyn to dinner. 'I feel you're all so busy with
the campaign that you haven't had a quiet evening
with friends for a long time. John told me you hadn't
been very well, so I decided what you need is an
evening when nobody even mentions Chase Hey and
its imminent closure. What do you say?'

Robyn laughed. 'It's very kind of you. You could be
right—extreme fund-raising fatigue, you mean? I think
we're all suffering from that to some extent.'

'Then we'll make it at the end of the month. A nice
relaxing dinner before you all have to face yet more
fund-raising rigours of the Christmas parties.'

It was a pleasant thought as the wind moaned and
howled around the cottage. Robyn prepared herself
some home-grown potatoes, carrots and onions, and

made herself a Spanish omelette. Afterwards she sat quietly, reflecting on the past few weeks, glad she had come to terms with her physical infatuation for Paul, and was beginning to feel capable of coping with it. Ross's intervention had been upsetting, but neither of them had referred to it again.

The wind was making so much noise that when there was a knock on the door Robyn thought it was only something blowing about in the garden. Then the bell rang, and she got up quickly, wondering who would be calling on such a night.

Paul Howell-Jones marched into the cottage without being asked, slamming the door to keep out the blast of cold rain. 'I'm sorry to intrude when I haven't been invited,' he began, his voice dangerously polite, 'but I have to speak to you, Robyn.'

'Go ahead.' She didn't invite him to sit down. He was obviously happier to pace about the floor, his raincoat flapping behind him, just as his white coat did in the ward.

He turned to face her. She had never seen him so angry. 'You are succeeding in making a monkey out of me, all right,' he growled. 'Like an idiot, I thought I'd see what you meant by talking about your mad friend Jackie, so I did go down to the arcade after work.'

'I'm glad.'

'Robyn, I've never heard so much trash in all my life. All she talked about was force-fields, and channels of life-giving energy, and pools of light!'

'I expect it isn't easy to sum it up in a single chat, Paul. There's really no need to raise your voice.' Robyn tried to reason with him, disappointed that the visit had been a failure, but not wanting him to give up so soon.

'That's not why I came. While I was there I noticed a joiner putting up a new sign over one of the empty units. Do you know who is coming there, Robyn? Have you any idea? Well, I'll tell you. A chiropractor, that's who!'

Robyn took a deep breath. This wasn't going to be easy, but she had a ready reply. 'That should be helpful. The orthopaedic clinics have been crowded with people with chronic back pain. A chiropractor would ease the orthopaedic surgeons' workload, so that they can treat the more serious problems.'

His voice was even lower, 'You mean send innocent patients to a quack?'

'I understand they have a fairly extensive training.'

'License to cause untold damage to human beings, you mean? Robyn, I want to know who allowed this— this quack into the building of a respectable hospital!'

'Tom Gordon took responsibility for letting out the units.'

'Then he's off his trolley too. Gordon wouldn't do a daft thing like that.'

'Paul, why are you taking this so badly? Don't you think Tom Gordon knows what he's doing? This new chiropractor is probably someone quite good, with a reputation for getting results. Didn't you read in the medical Press about the latest two-year study? Chiropractors get better long-term results than conventional traction and analgesic therapy. It's in black and white. A genuine medical study, supervised by a London hospital. I thought you wanted proof before you made up your mind? Well, there it is. So please, either sit down and let me make you a coffee, or go and complain to someone else. It's nothing to do with me. Anyway, I think it's a good thing.'

'You would!' His comment was withering, and he saw her face change. 'I'm sorry. I didn't mean——'

'You'd better go, Paul.'

His tone changed. 'I'd be grateful for a coffee. I haven't eaten yet. I came straight here.'

'It's a good job your patients didn't see you, then, ranting and raving like some prejudiced madman.' She didn't move, facing him with blazing eyes. 'You can make your own coffee! You know where it is. I'm not your ward sister now, Paul—this is my house and you've been behaving badly.'

He stood then, and his raincoat settled around his rain-soaked trouser legs. 'I'd better go, you're right. I apologise. It was unnecessary to come to you—you had nothing to do with what made me mad. Well, not much. I don't know why—somehow, I just came here automatically. Sorry.'

She didn't reply, just went to the door and drew back the lock. As he passed her his eyes were very green, his hair and eyelashes still wet. He just nodded, and went out into the raging night. Robyn closed the door, but not before she felt a sting of pity for the lonely man going out alone into the rain, with nothing to look forward to but a lonely pub meal, and a stark hospital flat. It went against her northern hospitality to let him leave her house with not even a cup of coffee to warm him. She opened the door again, and took a step out into the rain. But the Lotus had its headlights on, and was just driving away, hidden at once by sheets of sleet.

She wondered what mood he would be in the following day. He had a morning clinic, so wouldn't be up to see his patients until lunchtime. In the meantime, Mr Swainson Black brought himself along to the ward to be admitted, and the occasion made Robyn forget her irascible consultant for a few moments. Black had lost a lot of weight since his operation, and a lot of his florid colour. But he was still self-important, very much aware that he was conveying an honour on the hospital by allowing them to look after him.

'Good morning, Councillor. If you'll come with me, we have your room ready for you.'

'Sister West—glad it's you in charge. Know I'll be treated properly, at least. The food's probably muck, though. Hospital food always is.'

Robyn was tactful. 'Our chef is quite good, Councillor. With our being a small hospital, we can buy local produce more cheaply, instead of buying in bulk from refrigerated warehouses. I think you'll be quite surprised.'

'I don't eat eggs, you know. Cholesterol and all that.'

'There's a choice. Nurse Grey will make sure you have a menu for lunch.' She beckoned to Sally, with a private wink. Sally was not overly fond of patients with depression and anxiety problems. She considered them spoiled malingerers. Robyn whispered, 'Now you do know who this is, Sal? If you win him over, we won't be out of a job in four months' time.'

Paul arrived at the ward, his face impassive, at about twelve-thirty. He greeted Robyn and Sally without warmth. 'Black in?'

'Yes, Doctor, but he's having his lunch. Doesn't want to be disturbed.'

'Well, for goodness' sake——!' But Paul stopped himself. 'All right. No need to see him right away. Have you done any temperature and BP?'

'Not yet, Doctor. We thought he would prefer you to do it for him.'

Paul gave her a hard look, unsure whether she was joking with him. A consultant do temperatures and blood-pressures? Yet, wearily, he nodded. In Councillor Swainson Black's case, the consultant would have to swallow some of his pride. 'I don't want him stuck in bed. He isn't ill. He must keep active during the mornings. He can have an afternoon nap.'

'Yes, Doctor.'

Fortunately, having the councillor in the ward had taken the edge off last night's quarrel, and Robyn was relieved to have nothing more said about it. She watched Paul from under her eyelashes, though, and felt guilty for turning him out into the storm last night. Yet why should she? He was a young healthy man, and he had been rude to her. She must make more of an effort to erase the memories of her total delight in his closeness and passion from her consciousness. Yet so many little things reminded her—the smell of his clean shirt as he leaned over her to check a drug, the way he smoothed his hair from his eyes, the glimpse of his close-fitting trousers when the white coat floated open as he walked.

Robyn drove to the large Georgian house belonging to John Crabtree, his hospitable wife Irene and their four exuberant children on the appointed date, looking forward to being in their relaxed company. Tom Gordon was there with his wife, and so were Mr and Mrs Sarmsworth, the eminent surgeon and his property-owning wife. Irene was handing round canapés while John poured sherry, when Paul Howell-Jones was ushered into the room by the eldest daughter, who was acting as assistant hostess.

Robyn must have realised that another single person would have to be invited to balance the table. Paul was the obvious choice. Yet he had mentioned nothing to her about it in advance, though he must have known Robyn was invited too. John Crabtree joked, 'Sorry to inflict you on each other, after you've worked together all week! But I expect you've learned how to get along amicably by now!'

'Oh, yes. Good evening, Robyn.' Paul was very cool.

Irene Crabtree, with more intuition than her husband, said quickly, 'Don't worry, Robyn, I've placed you at opposite ends of the table. We simply can't have anyone talking shop this evening.'

'Thank you.' Robyn gave her a grateful smile. 'I wonder if that is possible, in a medical group like this?'

Irene responded brightly, 'I wonder if there is such a thing as a collective noun for doctors? A consultation of consultants, perhaps? What do you say, Robyn?'

'I'm afraid my suggestions may not be as polite, so I'll pass on that one!' Robyn spoke lightly, but she saw Paul turn his head and give her what could only be described as a chilly look. He evidently read her unspoken thoughts better than the rest of the company. Robyn looked away, her heart sinking. How could she possibly enjoy a relaxing evening with Howell-Jones around?

However, good food and wine, and the warmth and generosity of their hosts, soon helped to lighten the atmosphere. Robyn was seated between Tom Gordon and John, with Paul at the other end of the long light wood table next to his hostess. It suited Robyn very well.

It was only when the party broke up, at around midnight, that she found herself with a flat tyre. 'I'll drive you home.' And yet again she sat in the scarlet Lotus in silence. 'John will call the garage for you in the morning.'

'It's kind of you.'

'Not kind. Anyone would have done the same.'

'Thank you anyway.'

He looked at her sideways. 'Enjoy the evening?'

'Very much.'

'Notice how I managed to keep quiet about all the things that are bugging me?'

'Don't start, Paul? Please don't start now?'

'I'm not going to. But I thought you might have given me a little credit for tact.'

She said quietly, 'Oh, very well done, Paul. But I knew you wouldn't. No one could have been mean enough to spoil such a meal, and such hospitality. Not even you.'

Another sidelong look, but he didn't rise to the bait. Instead he said thoughtfully, 'They are a lovely family. Makes you feel a bit like an outsider, doesn't it? Seeing such happiness and togetherness. Those kids are delightful.'

'I do believe we're going to agree on something tonight.'

He drew up at the gate of Meadow Cottage. It was cold, with a hint of glistening frost on the roof and on the bare branches. He turned off the engine. 'Here we are.'

'Thank you very much.' Should she invite him in?

He said, 'See you on Monday, then. Back to buttering up Mr Black?'

No, she wasn't going to invite him in. With a sweet smile, she agreed. But her voice was acid. 'Each in our own different way, of course.' And she let herself out before he could open the door for her.

He lowered the electric window. 'You do realise that you could be suspended for disobeying my instructions? You're there to carry them out, not to read up superstitious little remedies of your own.'

'I wouldn't dream of disobeying you. I just add some personal touches to my nursing, that's all. I don't really expect you to understand. But I have been at this hospital longer than you, and a lot of patients have gone through my hands without making any complaints about the way they've been treated.'

It wasn't cold. It was very still, and the sky was studded with stars. A wintry moon, almost full, hung, glowing, in the velvet night. Robyn stood, looking down at Paul's face, framed by the car window. He was looking at her with a new expression, and she sensed his sudden change of mood. She wanted to turn away, but somehow didn't want to break the bond between them—even though it was a bond of argument and bad temper. He said, casually, 'I don't quarrel with that, Robyn.'

She replied quietly, 'Then it must be the only thing you don't want to quarrel about, Paul.'

He was looking up at her, his eyes shining in the light of the stars. There was something yearning and sincere in his voice as he said, unexpectedly gentle, 'You seem to be part of this sky, you know. Dark and calm and somehow very permanent. You've always been a night person, haven't you, Robyn? Always at home in the moonlight?'

Calm? Perhaps Mary's advice had begun to work? Robyn managed to smile a little as she looked into his eyes. 'Just at home in Barnaby, Paul, that's all. Maybe one day you might understand what it means to me.'

CHAPTER NINE
December

'I DON'T want to stay in this confounded place any longer, Sister West.'

Mr Black was not happy. Robyn was not happy because Mr Black was not happy. She tried to calm him. 'Dr Howell-Jones wanted to check your blood again. And he thought you might be interested in doing a few memory tests for him. The psychologist feels that you would benefit from a full profile of your mental capabilities. He thinks you might have lost your self-confidence. . .' Even as she spoke, she knew the psychologist would do less good than her own sister Mary in that field. Yet Paul had told her to get the psychologist. And, in this ward, Paul was God. Robyn said sadly, 'I do understand how you feel, Mr Black. I'll tell Dr Howell-Jones, shall I?'

'I'll tell him myself. Get him to come up, would you?'

Robyn tried to stay tactful. She knew Paul had an out-patients clinic, and would be furious if summoned to Mr Black's bedside in the middle of it. 'I'll see if he's in the building, Mr Black. Meanwhile, a nice cup of tea?'

'Why is tea always a nice cup?' complained the councillor, shifting petulantly in his chair. 'Why don't you just ask me if I want some tea?'

'Do you?'

'No, I don't.'

Robyn looked at him with a mixture of pity and irritation. The poor man had been through a lot since that fall from Napoleon at Willy Bragg's. Ross had discovered that it was Napoleon. 'Maybe you'd like to take a walk? You could go down to the café in the arcade, Mr Black. It's against the rules, but I'll bend them a bit for you. The ladies down there do some lovely snacks, and it might cheer you up a bit until I can get hold of Dr Howell-Jones.' If he was discharging himself anyway it would do no harm to let him go for a ramble inside the hospital. The whole-food prepared by Jilly and the two apple-cheeked girls in the arcade was probably better for him than cups of sweet tea anyway.

'What if he comes up when I'm gone?'

'I'll come and get you, I promise.'

It was with relief that she watched his shrunken form, in clothes that were too large for him, shuffle off without thanking her. At least she could concentrate on some of her other patients now. And she could see Sally was very relieved to see him go. 'You sure he'll be all right?' Sally asked.

'Quite sure. He's not daft. Just depressed.'

Sally shook her head, unconvinced. 'He's just not trying to get over it.' She noticed Robyn's look, and said with a grin, 'I know—I lack compassion for the afflicted! But you must admit he'd try the patience of a saint.'

'I admit it, Sal—I admit it. I just wish it wasn't so important for us to get him on our side. If we fail to cure him now. . .' She left the implication unsaid. They all knew what would happen to Chase Hey when spring came.

Philomena Gorsey called Robyn, in her quiet, undemanding voice. 'Sister, I wanted to tell you—Kevin's come back.'

Robyn searched her face for a clue to her feelings. 'And you still. . .?'

'He heard about the baby. He wants me to go to Salford with him. He's got a place we could live.'

It sounded hopeful, but Robyn still couldn't tell how she felt. With a sudden jolt, she realised that Phil was looking to her for advice. Was Kevin good or bad news? She said, 'Would you like me to have a talk to Kevin when he comes in to visit you tonight?' And the beam of relief told her she had said the right thing. It wasn't easy, being a substitute aunt, but Robyn was no longer afraid of saying the wrong thing. It was so often the case that she was merely a friendly ear, and the patients made up their own minds after talking freely with her.

Robyn was helping the physios with her stroke patients when Paul arrived in the ward. She was getting used to his coolness with her, but it still hurt a lot. She said as calmly as she could, 'Oh, Doctor, I'm afraid Mr Black has had enough.'

'What do you mean, enough?'

'He wants to go home.'

'But there's plenty we can still do for him. Where is he? I'll have a word.'

'I'll go and get him.'

'Where are you going?' His voice was dangerously calm.

'I let him go for a ramble, to keep his spirits up.' She began to realise she had been a little premature. Mr Black hadn't been discharged by a consultant, yet she had allowed an in-patient to leave the ward without permission. 'It was my decision. He was disrupting the care to the other patients.'

'Where did you send him?'

'To the café in ——'

'The arcade, I knew it! My God, Sister, what do you think you are doing, sending my patient into that place, where he could pick up all sorts of crazed ideas? He'll probably go to the chiropractor while he's there.'

Robyn's temper flared. 'And what harm would that do him anyway? I sent him for a snack, that's all.'

'So you're the doctor now, are you?'

'No.' It was a mild misdemeanour, and she ought to apologise. 'I was wrong to do it without your permission. But I'm sure——'

'Perhaps you'd like to prescribe for him too? Oil of jasmine, is it? Or maybe a little tincture of ylang-ylang?'

'There's no need to be sarcastic.' She added rebelliously, 'And it would probably do him more good than sitting here grumbling!'

'I want Mr Black here in two minutes, is that clear?'

But there was no need. Christopher Swainson Black was already ambling back into the ward, with wholemeal scone crumbs on his pullover, and a racing paper in his hand. 'Ah, there you are, Howell-Jones. I wanted to see you.'

'And I wanted to see you. Back into your room, please. At once. You're still under medical supervision, whatever else Sister West has led you to believe.'

Mr Black was in a better mood. 'You know, it's a damn good idea, that arcade. Decent food, and a few shops. Makes a nice change from being stuck in a square room all day looking at the lavatory door.'

Robyn ventured to add, 'And the rent comes in very handy towards our campaign, sir.'

Paul took Black's arm, and led him back to his room. Robyn nodded for Sally to go with them. She had had quite enough of Paul that morning.

When Paul came to her room later in the day, Mr Black had already gone home. Paul was calm, with no trace of the bad temper of the morning. 'I'm disappointed he left. I thought the psychologist might help. He's just frightened of life more than he used to be. I'm positive we'll get him better in time. Ah, well, I'll just have to do it in Out-patients. Can you get him back to my clinic the first week of January, please, Robyn?'

Robyn made a note to get an appointment sent before the Christmas rush of mail. 'Are you going home for Christmas?' she suggested hopefully.

'I might manage a weekend this month. I have to be here for the events—carol service, party and the Boxing Day fiesta. It's going to be an exhausting week. But the Christmas spirit might loosen a few more wallets in our favour, so it has to be done.' He sat down opposite her, and rubbed his eyes wearily.

'You're working too hard.'

'Not really. I can stand the pace, you know. Only I've got an appointment this afternoon with your uncouth newspaper friend. Sort of kiss and make-up meeting, so that things won't be awkward when he comes to the events. We still need every ounce of Press publicity we can get.'

'Did you ask for the meeting?'

He looked at her with a half-smile. 'I did. I'm not proud, where the success of the campaign is concerned. I don't mind the odd beating-up in a good cause.'

She shook her head slightly. 'I don't understand you at all, you know. You can be so tolerant and placid at times. Yet you fly up in the air when it's least expected.'

He grinned then. 'It's my fiery Welsh ancestors, I'm afraid. I've got a quick temper, and I've never quite managed to civilise it. Maybe it's part of my charm?'

'What charm?'

He put his elbows on the desk, and put his chin on his folded hands as he looked hard at her. 'We've not given each other an easy time, Robyn.'

'Are you blaming me?'

'I can't be all bad—can I?'

This was when she should have told him the truth. But instead she remembered some of the good times they had had, some of the nice things he'd said, and how many times she had felt sorry, or sad for him, being a loner in a bare hospital flat. 'Not all bad.'

He smiled. 'I'll have to settle for that, then. I was hoping for compliments.'

'When you shouted at me as if I were a naughty schoolgirl this morning?'

Paul looked at her. 'With justification, Robyn. I don't shout at people who don't deserve it.' But he had the grace to look away under her earnest gaze. 'I could have spoken more quietly. In private. Sorry.'

'And it may have done some good, sending Black down there. See how enthusiastic he was when he came back?'

'And how quick you were to remind him of the financial gain too!' Paul leaned back in his chair, and gazed out of the window at the calm winter landscape, with its muddy fields and bare trees. 'The fact remains that the rules are there. I'm responsible for that patient. I know you personally aren't likely to make a wrong decision, Robyn, but when we work in a structured environment we have to stay inside that structure.'

'Yes, I know. You put it so well now—so reasonably. If only wild Owen Glendower, or whoever it is in your Welsh ancestry, didn't have such an effect on your temper!'

He reached out his hand suddenly and put it over hers. They hadn't been in physical contact for some time, and the effect was electric. Robyn felt her cheeks grow warm as he said, 'I'm truly sorry. I'll try harder next time.'

'There may not be a next time.'

He smiled again. 'You mean Sister West is going to become meek and mild? Not likely!' He withdrew his hand. 'I'd better go. Shall I give Mr Cartwright your kind regards?'

She disregarded his playful lift of the eyebrows, and said firmly, 'Say nothing at all about me to Mr Cartwright.'

'OK.' He stood up. 'Take care, my dear.'

It sounded so nice and friendly, that 'my dear'. They'd used to be friendly. She wondered why he had become so quick to criticise lately. Perhaps it was something personal, something to do with Victoria. In that case, she had no right to ask. It was none of Robyn's business.

She would have been very puzzled if she had seen Paul Howell-Jones that evening. He was sitting at a corner table in the Three Bells, and with him sat Mary West, Amos Bridge and Ross Cartwright. Their heads were very close together, and they talked earnestly for a long time.

The carol service in the local church was packed to the doors, and when the vicar announced that there would be a collection for the hospital after the service the congregation, as Paul had predicted, were generous with their paper money. Mary and Robyn went together, and left before the others. Mary noticed that her sister was in a hurry to get away, but she made no reference to it. Mary West was not blind where her sister was concerned. She smiled secretly to herself, and later she telephoned Amos, and they had a long conversation.

On Christmas Day the doctors and nurses and their families went round the wards, singing carols, and giving presents to the children. Robyn had volunteered to be on duty, as the other girls had families to be with, and Mary had been invited to spend the day with Amos and his old mother. It was the first Christmas the sisters hadn't been together, but somehow neither regretted it, or even commented on the fact. Mary had been spending a lot more time with Amos—and, though it was possible he was merely giving her hints on growing a better herb garden, Robyn was inclined to think it was the gardener, not the garden, that was the attraction. Anyway, Robyn liked working on Christmas Day. The atmosphere was relaxed, and the only doctors around were the ones who came to sing.

The Boxing Day extravaganza, the fiesta, was held in the arcade, which was beautifully decorated and lit. Tom Gordon, whose idea it was, had entered into the spirit of the Caribbean totally, and laid on a steel band, and everyone was expected to dress up as brightly and as exotically as possible. Ross Cartwright, cheerful and well-mannered as though he had never tried to knock out Paul Howell-Jones, stayed quite close to his pretty photographer. They thoroughly enjoyed themselves, as normally staid and modest little nurses and secretaries wiggled their hips in sambas and merengue, in sequinned dresses and ornamented head-dresses. There was noise, and laughter, music, brilliant decorations and eccentric costumes, and everyone considered Mr Gordon's idea a brainwave, and one that ought to be repeated every year.

Robyn hadn't spoken to Ross since the incident. They came face-to-face while Robyn was dancing with one of the housemen, her Spanish-style flounced dress twirling over several lace petticoats. After the dance Ross drew her on one side. 'I'm sorry for being a lager-lout.'

'It's forgotten, Ross.'

'I'll never forget what a damn fool I made of myself. You know why, don't you?' She knew he was going to tell her, and felt suddenly uncomfortable. He went on, 'I've been—I've fancied you for months. I made friends with Mary, so that I could get to know you.'

'I didn't know. You didn't say anything.'

'I knew there was no point. I saw what there was between you and Howell-Jones.'

'There's nothing—he's got a girl—you know about him and Vicki Alexander—a top-earning model. One of the biggest. You think there would be anything between Paul and me with a girl like that around?'

'She's beautiful, I know. But she's hard too. Made of glass. Nothing inside.'

'Paul doesn't think so. They're buying a house together.'

Ross was being called by his photographer. 'I didn't know that. Surely not. How could he. . .? See you later, Robyn.' He was dragged away, but not before Robyn saw a light of contentment in Ross's eyes as he tucked his arm through his photographer's. Robyn wondered whether Ross had heard a word of her denial.

Mary was sitting with Jackie outside their shop, which was decorated beautifully with pale blue frosting and large blue baubles. She said, 'I saw you talking to Ross.'

'I'm sorry——'

'Don't be. I'm over it.'

Robyn watched her, and saw that she meant it. Even when the dancing became frantic, Mary didn't seem envious of those who could dance. She tapped her fingers on the arms of her chair, and clapped and cheered with the rest when the dance was over. It must be wonderful to have the ability to find that inner calm that shone in her pretty face.

Tom Gordon was elbowing his way over between groups of flushed and happy dancers. 'Robyn, we're having a committee meeting in two days' time. We've taken so much money over this season that we need time to add it up and decide if we're going to get enough.'

'Does it look good, Tom?'

'Yes. It looks good. But Paul has just told me about Black's taking his own discharge. That can't be good news, I'm afraid. I believe the district health authority is meeting in full session on the seventh of January. I wonder if they have an unpleasant little New Year gift for us, in spite of all our work.'

'They can't! Black promised not to make his mind

up until the end of the financial year. They hold the critical meeting in March.'

Tom nodded, and, raising his voice above the band, he said, 'But he still has the final decision, Robyn. All we can do is keep our fingers crossed.'

'I'll do that, Tom!'

'Bless you, you've done more than anyone, having the health authority people round as you did. If we lose I'll feel more sorry for you than for myself, you know.'

'We haven't lost until the final shutters go up, so let's not talk like losers. We're going to be winners, Tom!'

'Winners!' He put his thumb up. But his eyes were grave. Robyn took his hands, and led him into a gyrating merengue that left them both flushed and breathless.

It was late when Paul announced the last dance, thanked everyone for coming, and said they had all been too generous, but would they please go on being too generous until March the thirty-first! Robyn watched him affectionately. He was mercurial in temper, and set in his ways over some things. But his fire and his dynamism were what had kept this campaign going without flagging, and he had worked harder than anyone. As the applause died down, and the band prepared to play, she called out suddenly, 'Three cheers for our chairman! Hip, hip——'

The cheers echoed round the arcade, followed by a frenzied bout of applause. Then the music started. Suddenly Paul was beside her, drawing her into his arms. 'I haven't danced all night. Will you be my partner?'

'You know I will.'

'I wasn't expecting cheers—especially from you.' He had to hold her close, because the dance-floor was crowded. 'But it was the nicest surprise I've had all Christmas.'

'You were pleased about Philomena getting herself engaged. That was a nice surprise, wasn't it?'

'I think you know what I mean. I mean about us.' She said nothing. It had been a tiring few days, and she was content to nestle in his arms, her cheek against his shoulder. Gradually she realised that his grip was tightening around her, that they were hardly dancing at all, but standing in the middle of the dancers in a fervent and very satisfying embrace. This was something she had promised Victoria wouldn't happen. But while it went on somehow Robyn had no strength at all to bring the clinch to an end. Only when the music trailed to a finish, and people started clapping and cheering again, before Paul released her from his arms he bent his head and kissed her very deliberately on the lips.

She went back to Mary, still blushing. As she walked towards her sister she saw other faces—Ross Cartwright, John Crabtree with Irene, Jackie Darcy, Sally Grey—and she knew they all had seen the kiss, and all must know how besotted she still was with Paul. But she tried not to show it. 'Ready for home, Mary?'

'I'm ready.' Mary's face was subdued, but there was a knowing look in her eyes.

'Back to reality tomorrow.'

'It's been such fun. I do hope they'll have a fiesta next year. What an opportunity to let your hair down!'

Robyn said sadly, 'That depends on whether there'll be a hospital next year.' She pushed Mary's chair towards the car park, calling greetings and goodbyes as they went. Robyn said, 'It didn't mean anything, you know.'

Mary said quietly, 'I'm sure you're right.'

And she was. Next morning, Paul came into the ward with his usual busy expression. He started on the ward-round immediately, and talked of nothing but work, pointing out to the new houseman some interesting syndromes he might not have come across in his student days. Robyn walked behind, content not to be noticed. Then one of the patients called across the ward, 'Did you have a nice Christmas, Doctor?'

Paul looked up from his notes and smiled. 'Yes, thank you, Mrs Noakes. One of the best,' and he turned in a single second to look at Robyn. By the time she realised it he was already looking back at his notes. And the houseman hadn't noticed a thing. Robyn could only think of that kiss—the kiss in the middle of the arcade, in full view of just about everyone they knew. Was that what Paul's knowing glance meant? He didn't look at her again, and she had no way of knowing. But in her heart she hoped she knew.

Back in the office, Robyn put the kettle on. The new houseman, an earnest young man destined for great things, was questioning Paul closely. 'You think that Kawasaki's Syndrome will come up in my membership exam?'

'If it isn't in the papers, you'll probably get it in the vivas.'

The houseman made scribbled notes. Paul turned casually to Robyn. 'You know we're only five thousand pounds short of the target? Not bad for only nine months.'

'We've honestly raised over three hundred thou-

sand? It's a tremendous amount. I think you deserved
your cheers.'

He nodded, apparently dissatisfied. 'Yes, maybe.
Pity about old Black, though. Getting him well would
have made it almost a cert.'

'Don't blame anyone. It was a long shot anyway,
having him in. It's just one of those things.' As she
watched Paul she wondered why he was turning away
from her, as though hiding a smile. . .

As she walked to her car that evening, in the chilly
dusk, she noticed a smart little sports car outside the
doctors' quarters. She thought nothing more than one
of the housemen had treated himself to a new car, and
that he must have a rich daddy, because it was a
gleaming white BMW.

But the white sports car overtook her on the main
road home, and when she drew up at Meadow
Cottage, it was parked outside the gate. When she
stepped out of her car and locked the door, Victoria
Alexander got out of the BMW and locked it. Her
white-blonde hair shone in the light of the street lamp,
and the heels of her elegant boots clicked on the stones
of Robyn's front path.

Robyn took a deep breath. Paul must have asked
Victoria up north for the New Year celebrations.
'Hello, Victoria.'

'May I come in?'

Robyn shrugged. 'Yes.' She could hardly turn the
woman away. 'Is there something special you want?'
She turned the key in the lock and went in. There was
a savoury smell from the kitchen. 'Here I am, Mary.'
She turned to Victoria. 'Come in, won't you?'

'Hi! I'm all floury. Be through in a jiffy,' Mary
called.

'No hurry.' Robyn took her coat off and hung it up. Then she went through to the fire, and gestured Victoria to sit down. The model was wearing a slim white tweed suit and matching white leather boots. Robyn looked down at her own dark blue uniform, the firelight reflected in the silver buckle of her belt, and smiled to herself at the contrast. She said again to Victoria, 'Is there something special you want?'

The girl tossed her shining hair from her face. 'Not something. Someone special.'

Not again. The same old tune. Robyn said casually, 'Don't we all?'

'Don't pretend you're the innocent this time, Robyn. I heard about the Boxing Day party. You were all over him, I'm told. You promised to leave him alone!'

Robyn sighed. 'Can I offer you a drink? No? Well, I want one.' She poured a glass of Madeira, and sipped it. 'Victoria, telling me to leave Paul alone is like telling a pussycat to leave a bull terrier alone! Believe me. I wasn't all over him. We hardly saw each other the entire night. In fact it was the final dance, after he had finished being compère, that we danced just one dance. We—wished each other the compliments of the season. Why anyone should take the slightest notice of one kiss, when everyone was doing the same thing, I can't think. You must have highly imaginative spies, to make an incident about one kiss.'

'I may be imaginative, but from what I hear it wasn't just a simple kiss.'

Robyn was getting tired of being blamed for Paul's behaviour. She put her glass down and faced the glamorous vision on the sofa. 'Vicki, let it go, please? I have no intention of chasing your young man. We're friends—sort of, and we work together. If I wanted to make love to him I would think it was his decision whether to welcome my advances. It certainly isn't anything to do with you what I do in my own time with a man who is *compos mentis* and totally in control of his own life.'

'I happen to think it is. I happen to know that he thinks you're very beautiful, and have the loveliest eyes in the world.'

'Good heavens, do you? How do you know that?'

'Because he told me, damn you!'

Robyn retreated to a chair and sat down. She knew what it was like to have your feelings bruised by a man. She said gently, 'Can I tell you something else? I think he's very handsome, and his eyes are very attractive too. But he's also a pompous bully at times, and, however good-looking someone is, if you spend your time together always arguing and fighting then you haven't really got something going between you, have you, Vicki?'

Victoria Alexander's beautiful eyes were suddenly serious. 'I've known him a long time—he was proud to be seen with me when he was a student.'

'I can imagine.' She knew how the boy from the Welsh valleys felt about his humble background. Vicki's classy presence and devotion must have given Paul a lot of confidence he didn't have before. 'You helped him a lot, I'm sure. I know he appreciates you. But he's grown up now, and if he's grown away as well, I don't think it's because of me, Vicki. Truly, I don't.' It wasn't easy to explain, with Vicki's eyes searching her face, but Robyn made a heroic effort. 'I think he needs space, from both of us, but especially you, because he feels a sense of obligation to you. I'm trying to do my bit. I don't think Paul is the sort of man any woman can manipulate. He has to make his own life, and I'm not aiming to be a part of it. Until he does, it might be a good idea for us both just to be glad we're his friends. As far as I'm concerned, that's all I want.'

Victoria was silent for a moment, thinking hard. 'You're telling me to let him go. Don't you think that if you want something you should fight for it?'

Robyn looked down, suppressing the start of a smile. 'For this crazy Welshman? You've got to be joking.' But as Victoria turned away, apparently satisfied, Robyn's heart ached with trying to pretend she didn't want to fight for him. She said quietly, 'You could fight forever—but Paul Howell-Jones will still go his own sweet way. You know that, Vicki, I'm sure you do.' But she knew she still nursed those tendrils in her inner self, the tendrils of love that Paul had been the first man ever to awaken.

CHAPTER TEN
January

MARY WEST limped slowly but perkily from her bedroom on her calipers. 'Come on, Bobbie, hurry up. I know it isn't midnight yet, but let's not miss all the fun.' She was wearing a midnight-blue velvet dress, with a fitted bodice, a square neckline and full sweeping skirt.

Robyn, still in a tracksuit, followed her into the living-room. 'Look, Sis, I'll drive you. I know it's New Year's Eve, but I really don't feel much like going out. I need an early night, I think.'

Mary said equably. 'Suit yourself. But I hate to think of a West staying away from a party because she was intimidated.'

'Hardly intimidated!' Robyn smiled ruefully. 'Only warned off. Surely a woman as gorgeous as Ms Alexander should have more faith in her own ability to hold on to a man?'

Mary agreed as she eased herself into her wheelchair and smoothed down the gathers of her skirt. 'It was nothing to do with you if Paul Howell-Jones didn't go up to London to visit the girl last month. He had plenty to keep him busy here.'

'She didn't believe me, either, when I told her that I did nothing at all to encourage him. I wish I knew how she got hold of that copy of the *Recorder* with our photographs in.'

Mary smiled. 'But it was a good photo, wasn't it?'

'Oh, very flattering,' said Robyn scathingly. 'The only time we went near one another all night, and someone—naming no names—has to go and take a picture of us.'

'Kissing,' added Mary, with another smile. 'If you don't hurry up and get into something more glamorous we'll miss out on our quota of kisses at midnight.'

'You're in a very good mood tonight, Sis. Is there someone at the village hall you particularly want to meet?'

'If you want to know, yes.'

Robyn felt immediately contrite. 'You should have told me earlier, Mary. Here am I, busy with my own little problems, when I should have been thinking of yours. I'll be three minutes!' She was already pulling the sweatshirt over her head as she ran back into her bedroom. She looked hastily in the wardrobe. 'Do you mind if I wear velvet too? I think the slinky black with huge pearl earrings would be nice.'

'Perfect. Specially with being so slim after losing your appetite over Paul Howell-Jones.'

'It wasn't over——' But Robyn didn't bother to deny it to Mary. Instead, she zipped up the black sheath, scrabbled in the drawer for some sheer black stockings, and rubbed a hankie over her best patent black shoes to give them a quick shine. She brushed her hair, which needed cutting and swung like a heavy glossy curtain to her shoulders. Then she inserted her costume pearl earrings, which glowed like moonlight under her hair. 'Come one, then. It isn't quite ten yet. You shall go to the ball, Cinderella. And in my white Suzuki chariot into the bargain! Sorry it hasn't been to the car-wash for a while!'

At the door of the village hall they paused and

looked at each other. Mary said, 'She probably won't be there at all. Even if she is, it isn't any of Vicki Alexander's business if you want to go to a village hop in your own town. Forget the woman, Bobbie. It's your life, OK?'

'You're right, of course. And this is the beginning of a whole new year. I feel tons better after reading Jackie's book—and after all the advice you've given me, Sis. I'm as good as the next girl, and I think I believe it.'

'Great. That's what I like to hear.' They were inside now, in a hall where flashing lights made corners of brightness and deep shadow. Robyn felt safe enough staying in the shadows until she orientated herself. But Mary was immediately claimed by Amos Bridge.

'Thought you weren't coming.'

Robyn watched as he took over the wheelchair with a sudden fierce pride, and found them a corner where they could watch the dancing until a slow number that Mary could manage, held in his strong sturdy arms. Amos had been around to the cottage a lot more than usual recently, in spite of its not being the growing season. For the first time Robyn began to wonder what would happen to Meadow Cottage if one of the West sisters married. Neither would turn the other out. Yet the cottage wasn't big enough for a lodger.

As though echoing her thoughts, someone said behind her, 'Robyn, have you ever thought of selling Meadow Cottage?'

She recognised Victoria's voice, and it was a lot more friendly than at their last meeting. Paul must have talked his way out of not visiting her in London. She turned. Victoria was wearing something long-sleeved, in sequinned dark green, the neckline slit low

at the front, and down to her waist at the back. She
wore no jewellery except a wide diamond-studded
belt, which showed her waist off to perfection. Robyn
said, 'You look very nice, Victoria.'

'You look pretty good yourself,' said the other girl,
almost petulantly. 'Didn't I always tell you you could
if you tried? What about the cottage? Don't you realise
you could get as much for that cottage as you've been
saving up for in the Chase Hey campaign?'

'Three hundred and fifty thousand? Nonsense,
you're joking. It's poky! And this isn't London, you
know.'

'No. But if you put a thatched roof on instead of
those slates, and sold in spring, when all the blossom
was out——'

'No chance. I'd only sell to my sister—and vice
versa, so don't bother asking Mary.'

'You're wasting a valuable asset. I'd be willing to
make an offer, you know. I've always wanted a cottage
in the country.'

So that was it. She wanted to keep an eye on Paul.
Robyn said casually, 'But Paul will be moving back to
London in April. His contract——'

'He's renewed it for four more years.'

Robyn put her hand to her throat, suddenly short of
air. 'Four—years?'

'I thought you were buddies,' said Victoria, sound-
ing a lot happier about Paul suddenly. 'So you don't
tell each other everything?'

'I did tell you, Vicki. We hardly speak outside work
and the campaign.'

'I think I'm almost beginning to believe you. Well,
Robyn, dear, he's signed on again. If Chase Hey closes
he'll be full-time at the teaching hospital. If it survives

he does two days at the teaching hospital. It's worked out just as he requested. I'm glad there's something you don't know about him.'

Robyn was sarcastic. 'I'm so glad you're glad.'

'So—give my idea a little thought, won't you? If you accepted my offer, you and your sister would be wealthy women.'

Robyn said wickedly, 'Barnaby's a long way from London for weekends.'

'Rubbish, darling—it's only just off the M6.' She spotted someone. 'Paul—Paul, sweetie, I'm over here!' And then she apparently wished she hadn't, as he came over, dashingly, Celtically handsome in his dinner-jacket and black tie, and stopped dead when he saw Robyn. He didn't speak—just looked at her and nodded his head in an embarrassed way, and took Victoria on to the dance-floor. Robyn watched them until they were swallowed up by the flashing lights. Somehow that embarrassed nod was more pleasing to Robyn than the most sweeping of compliments. She knew her appearance had startled him into silence, and it was something pleasant to think about while she watched someone else in his arms.

Someone touched her elbow. 'May I? I thought you weren't coming.'

'Yes, Ross. How are you?'

He led her into a space, where they danced. 'You look wonderful. The best-looking girl in the room. Everyone is wondering why you aren't married, you know.'

'Happy in my work,' said Robyn hastily, hoping Ross wasn't thinking of proposing tonight. She remembered first meeting Paul in the ward, when he'd asked her the same question. Well, she and Paul had met,

and made friends, fallen out again, made it up again—
and here he was, being cleverly and definitely removed
from temptation. Still, she knew she and Paul were
still firm enough friends for it to last a lifetime now,
married or not. Victoria couldn't take that away. 'In
fact, I'd hate to change anything just now. I like my
life the way it is.'

Ross smiled. He rarely smiled, and it showed off his
rugged charm. 'Well, that's the West sisters off my list
of eligibles, then.'

'Why Mary?'

'Have you looked at her lately?' Robyn looked
across. Mary had abandoned her wheelchair, and was
sitting beside Amos Bridge, whose arm was very
definitely round her shoulders as though protecting her
from all the world. Ross went on, 'Looks pretty serious
to me.'

'I think maybe you're right. Oh, Ross, aren't you
just thrilled? Isn't it wonderful for her?' Suddenly the
idea of Meadow Cottage loomed large. It was a shared
home—but the garden belonged almost exclusively to
Mary. And to Amos, whose solid kindness and skills
had helped Mary into the gardener she was today. It
was Robyn who would have to sell her half, and find
herself somewhere else to live. . .But it would be
worth it to see Mary happy.

Then, almost too soon, the door was thrown open
so that the church clock of All Saints could be heard
striking midnight. Five, six, seven—— All around her,
people were seeking out friends and lovers, holding
hands. Robyn saw Paul's brown head next to Victoria's
fair one, and suddenly felt tears burning her eyelids.
She turned, but the floor was crowded, and there was
nowhere to run to. Then Ross put his arm firmly round

her waist, and pulled her close. 'A substitute is better than nothing, Bobbie.' And, as the last note died away, he drew her into his arms. 'Happy New Year, love.' And after he kissed her he wiped away the tear that had escaped down her cheek. 'It's going to be all right, you know.'

'Happy New Year, Ross.' Suddenly she flung her arms round his neck and hugged him for being there, for being a friend. 'Happy New Year, everyone!' Streamers were being thrown everywhere now, and the kissing began. She managed to find Mary, whom Amos had steered thoughtfully out of the dance-floor back to her chair. 'Happy New Year, my dears.' She kissed them both, hardly needing to be told their news. It shone in their eyes. She supported Mary on one side, with Amos staunch on the other, through the singing of 'Auld Lang Syne'.

The dancing started again, and glasses of wine were handed round. So this was the year in which they would know the fate of Chase Hey. Robyn moved into the shadows, and watched the fun as an onlooker. Amos would see Mary home. She put down her glass, unwound a streamer from her neck, and slipped slowly outside.

'I thought you would be the first to run away.'

'Oh—Paul, I didn't see you there.'

'Just getting some air. Happy New Year, Bobbie.'

He stood alone, handsome and rakish with his hair ruffled, and his arms folded as he leaned against the porch. She repeated the greeting, meaning every word, before Paul reached out one hand to hold one of hers, and kissed her gently. She couldn't see Vicki, but she had to be there somewhere, waiting to pounce and protect. 'And good luck, Paul. I must go now.'

'Wait.'

'There isn't any point.'

They were very close, their hands and their clothes pressed together. The smell of him and the warmth of him seized her senses, caused the night to catapult her imagination into orbit. 'See you tomorrow?' Yes, as a friend, he would see her tomorrow, and the next day, and the day after that. Victoria could stake out her claim to him from here to eternity, but there was always friendship. She couldn't take that away.

She took her hand away, very gently. 'See you tomorrow.' She wouldn't say anything about his new contract. He would tell her when he was ready. 'Goodnight, Paul, and God bless you.'

She drove away quite quickly, so that he wouldn't notice her wiping her eyes. At the cottage she parked, and locked the car. Even in winter the garden smelt beautiful and familiar. Robyn felt a sense of loss, more than of a person, of a home. But it wouldn't be lost if Mary and Amos were here. It would always be a part of Robyn too. And who knew? The hospital might close, and she would have to go away anyway. She ought to be delighted that Mary would be always here, and Victoria Alexander wouldn't get her pink-tipped talons on Meadow Cottage forever.

Mary planned to marry in the spring. 'I want to wait until we know for sure that Chase Hey will still be open.' Mary's thoughts had run along the same lines as Robyn's. 'Until then, things will be just the same as always.' But they weren't, and never could be. Mary was constantly going over to Amos's smallholding, spending whole days there, and driving Jackie mad when she forgot to deliver new supplies to the shop in the arcade.

One day she had forgotten a whole consignment of lavender bags and pot-pourri, and Robyn had to take them over to the arcade before starting her own work. 'Don't be angry with her, Jackie. She deserves her happiness.'

'I hope it doesn't go on like this!' Jackie pretended to complain. 'I'll have to get a fellow of my own. I say, you know Mr Black has been back to visit me? Your Swainson Black of the district health authority?'

'Snooping, was he?'

'I don't think so. He said something about enjoying the atmosphere in here.' She waved her hand at the arcade, with its potted palms and weeping figs, the little tables and wicker chairs just being dusted and put out in the centre space, and the paintings by Jackie's friend, Nigel, for which he paid a commission to the hospital fund whenever any was bought. 'He certainly likes the food. He says Dr Howell-Jones has ordered him to take a walk every day—I think we're just far enough for him to be ready for his mid-morning snack when he arrives!'

'I wonder if he's beginning to appreciate Chase Hey?' Robyn scarcely dared to hope.

Jackie grinned cheerfully. 'I think it's Jilly's whole-meal scones he's appreciating at the moment. It's chilly, taking a morning walk in January. Her scones are straight from the oven.'

'Sell like hot cakes?' suggested Robyn, with a smile. 'Well, must get back to my patients. Funny how I was severely reprimanded for allowing Mr Black to come down, yet it's done him so much good. . .'

Jackie rearranged some of the books on natural and

complementary medicine on her display stand. 'Plenty to do folk good down here, if they care to come. But don't get yourself into trouble again!'

'By the way, how's the chiropractor?'

'You haven't heard? Doing very well. Originally he was keeping on his old premises in the village, but he's coming here full-time now. Word gets around, you know.'

She followed Paul and the keen houseman round the ward, listening to the kindly way Paul spared time to explain and to teach. Coffee-time these mornings was taken up by the two men talking about medicine, and Robyn was in a way quite grateful, because she recalled the tête-á-têtes they'd used to have, knew they were ancient history, and missed them very much.

It was Paul himself who came back to speak to her one morning. 'Have you time to have lunch with me?'

She had. Why pretend? They sat in the staff canteen, over soup and Jilly Forshaw's brown rolls. 'Something important?'

'Fairly. We won't be having any formal fund-raising from now on. The target isn't far off, and money keeps coming in from covenants and interest. But I was wondering—you used to tell me about Willy Bragg?'

'Yes—Mary and I were regulars on his ponies as children. Knew all the horses by name. He never changes, does Willy. Still thinks he knows everything there is to know about bloodstock.'

'I'd rather like to take a canter one day. Would you come with me, introduce me? I believe he's quite a character.'

'I'd love to. Are you a good horseman?'

'Like you, I used to be very keen. But med school

and housemanship don't leave much time for any hobbies. Shall we make it Saturday?'

'Are you——?' Robyn coloured. She shouldn't be interfering in his private affairs. If Victoria were indeed coming for the weekend, would Paul be asking her out?

But he understood. 'No engagements this weekend,' he grinned. 'And Vicki Alexander is in Paris for a summer promotion.'

'Summer?'

'Oh, yes. They have to promote summer clothes in winter and winter clothes in summer. Daft, isn't it?'

'Not daft, maybe—they have to prepare for the next season. But most uncomfortable, I'd think.'

'Are you glad you're a nurse?'

'Very glad,' smiled Robyn.

'So am I,' said Paul Howell-Jones.

Mary was curious. 'I don't see Paul wanting to ride for the sake of riding. Not in a bitter-cold month, with some of the worst weather to come.'

'Maybe he wants to be an outdoor type.'

'And maybe the mouse wants to play while the cat is away?'

Robyn gave her sister a long look. 'Are you warning me not to allow myself to be used? You think I can't look after myself, little sister?'

'Where Paul is concerned, I'm not sure that you can.'

'Look, I promise not to get hurt. I know what I'm doing.'

'I hope your fingers were crossed when you said that!'

Robyn arranged by phone with Mr Bragg. 'I'm

bringing a friend from the hospital. Tall chap, so don't give him Dinkums.'

'I'll give you a good horse, Robyn. See you on Saturday, then.'

When they drove over to Willy Bragg's farm Paul seemed much more interested in looking over the place. In spite of the cold, he insisted on walking round with Willy, praising his set-up, and admiring the view and the lay-out of the stables. It was only after meeting most of the horses that he consented to be mounted on a grey stallion called Lochinvar, while Robyn settled for a chestnut pony who rejoiced in the name of Polo Player.

They walked the horses for a while, ambling along the country lanes. But the wind was chill, and Robyn suggested a gallop. Paul said, 'I was interested in the old bay. Napoleon, you said his name was. That was *the* Napoleon? Handsome beast, but isn't he the one who threw Swainson Black?'

'So they say. But he's never thrown anyone viciously before. He's spirited, but not mean.'

'Has anyone asked Black what happened?'

'I don't know. Ask Sarmsworth. Ask Willy, come to that.'

'I might. I'm strangely curious about that incident.'

'We can't do anything about it now.'

'Probably not. Come on, Bobbie, let's go!' And he set off at a good canter, giving Robyn quite a job to catch up with him.

As they drove back to Meadow Cottage, he said, 'Lunch at the Bells?'

Robyn heard all sorts of voices telling her to say no. But it seemed silly not to, when Mary was out with Amos, and Paul was all alone too. 'Why not?'

'Good.'

They sat in the snug, drank halves of bitter and ate fish and chips. She said, 'Mary and I often used to do this.'

'Not now?'

'She's engaged.'

'I see. Too busy. Well, maybe you and I——'

'No, Paul.'

'Any good reason?'

'You treat me like a friend when it suits you, and turn away from me when it suits you. And you keep things from me.'

'Things?'

She sat still for a while. 'Why are you still living in the hospital flat?'

'Why not?'

'You see? You don't want to tell me your future plans.'

He seemed embarrassed. 'They're not really sorted out yet, Robyn.'

'You mean Victoria hasn't got herself a country cottage to be near you yet. But she will, won't she, Paul, now that you have a four-year contract?'

He looked down at his empty plate, until a waitress thought it was a hint, and came to take it away. 'You know how it is with these things. Plans are very fluid. Mary and Amos must find the same problems—there's so much to think about that's new and unfamiliar.'

'When you're planning a wedding, you mean?' Robyn looked at him hard until he looked up and faced her. His green eyes were very sincere, and crushingly handsome. How she hated the idea of Victoria Alexander at that moment. But she said,

'Amos? I don't recall telling you the name of Mary's fiancé. I assumed you would think it was Ross.'

'I did see them at the New Year party, Robyn.'

'Oh, yes, so you did.' But his reply didn't sound convincing. It was Robyn's turn to look down, disappointed in their lack of confidence in one another, as friends who had shown some regard for each other in the past.

He said, 'I was meaning to tell you about the contract. But, to be honest, I didn't want to see the look of horror on your face, at the thought that I might be around for another four years, when you thought you were getting rid of me in April.'

She smiled then, as he had intended her to. 'You think I would be horrified?'

He shook his head from side to side slowly, with a smile in his eyes. 'Just think—if I hadn't renewed my contract you might even have had a new consultant who likes your arcade and its pseudo-medicine. He might even have done a bit of acupuncture instead of doling out analgesics. And now you're stuck with me for another four years. It must be disappointing for you.'

She raised her eyebrows casually, pleased at his interest, pleased that he was looking at her as though it mattered what she said. 'Not really. Even the best of consultants has to be sorted out before he settles down. Better the devil you know——'

'Well, thanks very much! It isn't the most flattering of comments.' But he looked quite pleased too. . . That evening he was back at the same table, and while he spoke with Amos and Mary they all did a lot of nodding and smiling, and hands were shaken as though an agreement was being made.

CHAPTER ELEVEN
February

ON THE first damp and dreary day of February, Robyn woke with a feeling of challenge. Only a month to go until the health authority in the shape of Mr Swainson Black made the decision that would affect so many lives in Barnaby. She knew Paul was certain they had enough money to set up a trust fund for Chase Hey. But it wasn't just a matter of money. Not now.

Mary was already up, and there was the familiar smell of fresh toast and coffee. 'Rotten day for humans, Bobbie. But Amos says what's bad for humans is often good for the ground.'

Robyn was just as optimistic. 'Never mind the weather. We've got a month left to make it clear to Mr Black that Chase Hey is far too valuable to Barnaby to be closed, and that he'll be the most unpopular man in the entire world if he allows it to close. Think we'll do it?'

'You deserve to, Sis. Nobody has worked harder than you and Paul. I don't see what else you can do, these last weeks. I suppose the waiting is the worst part. Do you know when the health authority will hold the decisive meeting?'

'It must be about the seventeenth of March. They have to get their affairs in order before the end of the financial year, you see.'

Mary said, her face serious, 'You know how I feel about this place. I love it dearly. But my leaving it to

155

be married just at this time has put another worry your
way, just when you could do without it. I did think of
putting the wedding off until your future is more
certain. But——'

Robyn sat back and wagged her finger at Mary.
'Don't you dare talk like that. You've found a husband—one of the best—and that's the greatest thing
that could have happened, don't you forget it. I'm
thrilled and delighted and can't wait to be a bridesmaid. You are going to ask me to be a bridesmaid,
aren't you?'

'Who else?' laughed Mary. 'Talking of financial
years, we've set the date provisionally for the last week
in March.'

'That's great! Excellent choice. So, if we're all
depressed about the hospital, at least we'll have a
wedding to cheer us all up.'

Mary said tactfully, 'Will—Paul be around? Or will
he go to another hospital right away?'

Robyn swallowed a sharp crust of toast, and
coughed before answering. 'Any of the district hospitals would be lucky to get him. He told me the teaching
hospital. He's a wonderful teacher.'

Mary said with an air of wisdom, 'I honestly believe
he only agreed to renew the contract because he wants
to stay at Chase Hey. He wouldn't be happy anywhere
else.'

'Don't be fanciful, Mary. He's a consultant, not a
dreamer. Happiness doesn't come into it. Career structure does.'

'If you think so. . .'

'I know him, don't forget. Remunerative career
structure first. Then a home and a family—in that
order.'

'Do you think he'll marry Vicki?'

Robyn said shortly, 'He might. He could just be fool enough.' She looked around for her shoulder-bag and blue raincoat. 'Time I was off. Vicki is a self-centred girl. She would grace his dinner table for a few months—but she'd soon get tired of his irregular hours, and the way he goes back to the ward in the evening if he's worried about someone. She wants to be the centre of his life. I doubt if there's a doctor's wife in the world who could say that she was. It's the wrong profession for matrimonial togetherness. They all have to learn to share their men with a few thousand patients. No, Mary, it wouldn't suit Ms Alexander at all, once the glamour had worn off. Vicki is no Irene Crabtree.'

'I'll remember that,' said Mary, looking a little out-of-breath at her sister's vehemence. She looked after Robyn as she opened the front door, and took her car keys from the dresser. 'I won't——'

'Be in for dinner. How did I guess? Don't worry, Mary—I'll manage fine. I might even eat out. See you later, Sis.'

Paul was already in the ward when Robyn arrived. He was sitting at her desk, poring over a patient's file with the houseman, and checking X-rays. As usual, she felt a little lift of pleasure just looking at him and knowing they would be spending part of the day together—even if it was only looking after patients. He looked up briefly. There was a preoccupied look in the green eyes today. 'Hello, Robyn. I had to come in early. Want to get away sharpish after the clinic—something's come up.'

'About the hospital?'

'About the campaign funds. Tell you all about it when I get back.'

He was frowning slightly, but she dared not question him any further while they saw patients, and once the round was done he was away with his flying white coat tails to start his out-patients clinic. The houseman said meekly, 'Do we not get a coffee when sir isn't here?'

'I'm sorry, Rob. I'll put the kettle on. Do you know what's bothering him?'

The young man shrugged, and said cautiously, 'He took a phone call, and said "Oh, no!" in a furious voice, and banged the phone down.'

'I see. Bad news, then.'

'That's my diagnosis.' He coughed. 'I'm afraid I have more news for you. He told me to tell you that Philomena is back in hospital.'

Robyn sat down and put her head in her hands. 'What has she dreamed up to suffer from this time, Rob? And why isn't she in this ward? She always comes into this ward. It's her second home.'

When Rob didn't reply, she turned round to see him grinning broadly, his eyes twinkling behind his glasses. 'Paul asked me to explain that she's in Gynae— pregnant again. Nothing wrong, just in for a few days because of her morning sickness! Her boyfriend is delighted. She's asked for permission to have the wedding in the hospital chapel!'

She sat for a while after he had gone, looking out of the window at the drizzle. 'I hope she isn't still too attached to Chase Hey to break away and make her own life.' All her earlier optimism had drained away this morning, and she wondered what view she would be looking at a year from now. City streets? Rain- soaked Manchester roof-tops? Even on the drabbest

of days, Barnaby fields, and Willy Bragg's farmhouse
and outbuildings, were preferable to any other outlook. And when spring came, with the calves, the
lambs and the foals, the fresh green of the hedgerows
and the budding trees, there was nowhere in the world
she would rather be. And in Meadow Cottage, of
course. . .

She waited for news from Paul all day, but none
came. She tried not to think of what could have
happened—all the money stolen? A leaked letter from
Mr Black condemning Chase Hey for not having the
right equipment, for not curing his depression? When
her shift ended she didn't go home, but walked down
to the arcade to chat to Jackie, and have a cup of tea
and a slice of home-made fruit cake at Jilly's.

'Getting used to having the cottage to yourself,
Robyn?' Jackie came out of her shop and sat with her
in the café. 'I always thought you'd be the first to get
married. I suppose you and Mary had talked about
what would happen when that happened? Rose-hip
tea, please, Jilly.'

Robyn smiled thoughtfully. 'This last year has been
unsettling in so many ways that I was prepared for the
fact that I'd have to move. I'll find somewhere, no
problem. But it seems like sacrilege for us both to
leave it.'

'You'd only have to move if the hospital closes, so
don't fret until you have to. Mary will definitely be
moving to live with Amos and his mother, won't she?
After all, he can't leave his smallholding. It's his
livelihood. Mary's been talking of moving her herb
garden to a corner of his place.'

Robyn could have hit herself for not thinking along
those lines. 'You're right, of course. It's Mary who'll

be moving out, and I who will buy her half. If I'm staying in Barnaby. If not. . .' She paused for a while, her thoughts wandering. 'I don't know who will own Meadow Cottage if I go. Mary will miss the orchard.'

'Nothing to stop her planting a few fruit trees right there in the Bridges' place. They've plenty of land, you know.'

Robyn said, 'I suppose they have. It just—won't be the same.'

'Think about it,' said Jackie. 'And don't dare think about selling up just yet. I have a feeling you'll see quite a few more springs in your little garden. Here, have a flapjack with me?'

'No, thanks. I ought to get back. Paul might phone. . .' And she saw a flicker of gossip in Jackie's eyes. 'About work.'

When Paul did phone, it was after ten. 'There's been a problem with one of the covenants, Robyn. Someone had to pull out. Evidently he already owed the Inland Revenue some large amount when he offered us five thousand pounds. His heart was bigger than his bank balance.'

'You've been with the treasurer?'

'Yes, we had to revise all our figures. We're not quite as rich as we thought. We checked most of the others, in case anyone else has done the same. It's disappointing—but not the end of the line yet, Robyn.'

'Does this mean we have some more money-raising to do?'

'I can't quite see how we can raise that much in one month. I'll call a meeting in a couple of days, and we'll see if anyone has any bright ideas.'

Robyn said gloomily, 'Everyone has worked so

hard. We were winding down. It won't be easy to get the momentum going to start again.'

'Don't you think I don't know that?' His voice was sharp, and at once he apologised. 'I'm sorry. I'm a bit tired.'

She put the phone down slowly, and sat for a while, staring into the fire. A crazy idea came to her—that she would soon be the sole owner of a cottage, and that according to Victoria it could be worth quite a lot of money. If she sold Meadow Cottage she might save Chase Hey. She wanted Chase Hey to survive. Maybe she had been chosen by fate to save everything at the final moment? But dared she put this idea to Mary? Robyn went to bed without making a decision. She felt a new surge of hope. She needed time to think it through.

On Valentine's Day Robyn found her desk flooded by a pile of cards from her grateful patients. Laughing, she sifted through them, sure that there would be none from Paul, but hoping, just slightly hoping to catch sight of his familiar writing on one of the envelopes. Sally said, 'I wish I'd gone to the same charm school as you! I only got five!'

'Never mind, Sal. You're learning. I'm pleased with you—especially the way you managed to be patient with Mrs Wood. And dear little Phil. That was good training for Mr Black, wasn't it? Mr Councillor Black. He was a tough customer even for me to cope with.' She opened another evelope, and her eyes grew round. 'I say, Sal, come and look at this!'

It was a large card, with a sumptuous photograph of roses on the front. And inside was written, 'To Sister Robyn West and all her staff, with compliments and grateful thanks, C Swainson Black.'

The two nurses sat back in surprise. 'Do you think he really liked us, then?' Sally was turning the card round as though she could hardly believe the words.

'Looks like it. If he did, it was half your doing, Sally.'

'He must be feeling better.'

'That's just what I was hoping. He must have some warm feelings for us, to take the trouble to send this. It's giving me some good vibes, Sally. Let's just keep on praying!' Robyn looked at her watch. 'Look, I'm due for a break in a minute. Jackie says Mr Black is often at the café about eleven. I'm going down. If he's feeling grateful to the staff of Chase Hey—it changes a whole lot of things!'

'Don't ask him straight out, Robyn!'

'I'm not stupid. I'll just make polite conversation.' But Robyn found herself giving a little whoop of joy as she pinned the cards up around the notice-board, with Mr Black's roses in a prominent position.

Mr Swainson Black was indeed sitting at his favourite table with its little checked tablecloth, drinking lemon tea and eating a wholemeal scone with butter and damson jam. Robyn felt a little knot of apprehension as she walked in, and pretended to notice him just as she walked past. 'Why, Mr Black! How very nice of you to send us all a Valentine.'

She watched him as he laid his racing paper down and smiled up at her. He had lost his florid look, and one of his chins. Instead he looked pale but fit, and his eyes looked larger without the puffiness of poor health. 'Time for a cup of tea with me, Sister West?'

'That's very nice of you.' She took the chair he offered.

'I come here almost every day for my constitutional.

I'll miss it when I get back to my practice. It's become quite a little home from home.'

'You're back to the office soon, then?'

'Yes, Sister. Part-time, of course, but I need the interest now. It's been a long time, but I'm finally back to my old self—if not better than my old self.'

'I'll tell them in the ward. They'll be so pleased. Does Dr Howell-Jones know?'

'I have an appointment with him next week. He'll see for himself.' Black gave her a knowing smile, and went on, 'I admire the way that man has treated me, week after week, without once mentioning the campaign to save the hospital. I know he's the chairman, and has worked like the very devil to raise the money. But I'll say this for him—he knows what's medicine, and he knows what's business—and he knows they don't mix.'

Robyn bit her tongue, to stop herself asking about the final decision. 'You have been able to keep up with your health authority work, then?'

'Off and on, Sister. Off and on. Try one of these scones? They're quite excellent. Never used to eat wholemeal stuff. Now I like it better.'

'Was that on medical recommendation, Mr Black?'

'Not a bit of it. I found it out for myself when you first sent me down here to this arcade. Jackie in the herb shop made me welcome, and gave me a few leaflets to read.'

'Good for Jackie.'

He looked at her again, and she was delighted to see the transformation from testy and petulant patient to the capable lawyer he used to be. He said quietly, 'I've written to Dr Howell-Jones, asking him to send me all the facts about the money you've raised, and the arrangements you've made for a trust. The facts will be circulated to all my members, and we meet on the seventeeth, Sister. I promise you we won't come to a decision lightly. But we must consider all the facts, in the light of our government directive.'

He was being honest with her, and she appreciated it. But what if the money wasn't enough? Robyn said suddenly, 'I—I'm raising the money on Meadow Cottage, Mr Black, if we haven't got enough. That won't appear in the facts you'll be getting, because I haven't told Dr Howell-Jones about it. I need to talk to my sister and her fiancé.' She saw that time was passing and she ought to get back on the ward. 'I've got to go, Mr Black. But would you bear in mind that, whatever the official figures are, there'll be at least another five thousand from me?'

He was raising his eyebrows now. 'Better get it in the official figures, then, Sister. My members want hard facts, not promises.'

'I realise that. I'll do my best.' She went back to the ward rather breathless—not because she had been hurrying, but because she had been worrying. What if Mary wouldn't allow the sale to go ahead? Robyn knew she had been hasty in telling Black. But what else could she do on the spur of the moment?

Paul was in her office. She sat down after a murmured greeting, feeling guilty. She couldn't tell anyone else her decision until she had spoken to Mary. She ought to speak to Mary at once, and confess what she had done. But she didn't know where Mary was. Paul said, 'You're daydreaming, Sister.'

He had been speaking and she hadn't taken any notice. 'I'm terribly sorry. I didn't hear you.'

'I know you didn't. I said that I notice it's

Valentine's Day.' He indicated all the cards with a smile. 'You're a popular young woman.'

'They're really for all the staff,' she said hurriedly. And she pointed out the big one from Mr Black. 'I've just been speaking to him.' She repeated what Black had said.

Paul sat back. 'It doesn't sound too bad, then. I'm cautiously optimistic, as they say. If the figures are right, I believe we've made enough friends among the other members of Black's board. We've invited them free to all our functions, taken them on tours of the hospital, given them the run of your lovely cottage, and fed and watered them as well as we possibly can.'

'I wish we didn't have over a month to wait.'

'You sound quite agitated. That's not like you, Robyn. Are you all right? Is there something else you want to tell me?'

'I'll be all right.' She looked up at him, her eyes troubled. Paul seemed affected. Suddenly he put his hand on her cheek, and bent and kissed her. 'You look scared, Robyn. I've never seen you so vulnerable. Want to tell me about it?'

Blushing at the sudden show of concern—she had never been kissed in her office before—she stammered, 'I—I can't. But thank you.' She pulled herself together. This would never do. 'Did you want Mrs Thwaite to have those iron injections?'

'I've already sorted that out with Rob. We've written her up, and he's given her the first jab. Anything else?'

Robyn opened her mouth to tell hm that she was in a position to help the campaign fund by as much as it wanted to reach its target. But she knew she had no right to speak, and closed her mouth again and pulled some papers towards her, sorting them out with nervous fingers. Paul put his hand on her shoulder. 'Well, I can't force you. Just don't forget I'm here if you want me.' And he squeezed her shoulder and left her. It was strange that, however much they might argue, Paul had always been there when she'd needed him.

Mary wasn't at home, and she wasn't at Amos's place. After four telephone calls, Robyn gave up. She would have to wait till Mary came home. She would have been highly suspicious if she had seen where Mary was that night. She was sitting in Paul Howell-Jones's small hospital flat, both of them at the table, with, opposite, the smiling figure of Christopher Swainson Black, holding a sheaf of papers, and a file full of documents. 'You know I can't influence the health authority either way, Miss West, but I can act for you in selling your half of the cottage. The trouble is, it can't be ratified until I get your sister's approval. I need her signature.'

'So I can't give her a surprise?'

He smiled again. 'Knowing you and your kind nature, I'm well aware that it would be a pleasant surprise. But the law is the law, designed to protect those who would rather do without surprises. Still, I can have all the necessary documents drawn up, so that when she finally has to know the sale can go right ahead.'

'It's very good of you, Mr Swainson Black.'

Paul drove Mary to Amos's house. 'It's subterfuge, but Robyn deserves something good to happen, and I want her to have it. She asks so little for herself. And you've been a source of great inspiration, you know, Mary. Thanks for agreeing to keep my interest a secret.'

Mary looked at him seriously. 'I'm trusting you, Paul. I've always trusted you.'

'You've been very decent to me, Mary. I was very much of an unbeliever when I came to you for help over Black's therapy. Can I say I'm very much on your side now? Treat the whole patient, not just the part that looks ill? I haven't told Robyn yet. She thinks I'm still an ogre.' He paused. 'But I get the feeling that she likes me a little.'

He was seeking reassurance. Mary nodded slightly. 'Oh, yes; a little, Paul.'

Robyn was still sitting at her desk and thinking of Paul, of his kiss, the sweet way he had touched her cheek, and kissed her with his warm lips. It was a brotherly sort of kiss. And she felt even more wretched then, because she knew how much she loved and needed him.

She drove home quickly, praying that Mary was in. But the cottage was in darkness, and Robyn lit the kitchen stove, reluctant to sit in the living-room by herself. She felt like a traitor, even thinking of putting up their little house for money. She heard a car engine, and ran to the door, expecting it to be Amos's van. It was Paul. She watched him with beating heart as he locked the car door and turned towards the cottage.

'I thought it might be Mary,' she explained as Paul raised his eyelids at seeing her on the front step in the porch.

'Is she missing?' His eyes were hooded.

'She's probably at the pharmacy with Amos. Jackie was needing some more stock, and it's quite a drive to Accrington.'

'Why are you still in uniform?'

She looked down, and shrugged. 'I—didn't realise. . . It doesn't really matter.'

'Whatever it is that's worrying you, forget it. I'm taking you out for dinner. Wear your black.'

'My black velvet? But that's too grand for the Three Bells. It's for parties.'

'Don't argue.'

'Why do you want to go out anyway? I'm not good company.'

'Bobbie, hurry up. I'm hungry. Anyway, if you must know, I want to thank you—for a lot of things. Can't you take a bit of gratitude, woman?' He always had a way of getting her to smile again. When he was being nice, he really knew how to be nice, how to treat a lady. She changed into her black dress, realising that he was wearing a smart suit with a matching waistcoat, and looked very handsome tonight. He said, as they closed the door and walked to the car, 'It's Valentine's Day, and there's a special evening laid on at the Royal Hotel. I thought—as we are both at a loose end tonight—that it would be nice to go together.'

'The Royal? That five-star place? I've never been there before. Are you sure you want——?' But Paul only smiled as he opened the passenger-door for her. Robyn shut up.

The Royal was a few miles outside Barnaby, and from the cars in the car park Robyn was sure there wouldn't be any room left for dinner. But Paul took her hand confidently, and they walked in, and were immediately welcomed by the head waiter. 'Good evening, Doctor, madam. Your table is ready.'

'You booked,' accused Robyn as they crossed the luxurious carpet and were escorted to one of the best tables at the side of the gleaming teak dance-floor.

The room was decorated with red glass hearts and silver streamers, and a pianist was playing soft music. 'Why did you pretend it was a spontaneous decision to come out?'

'I don't think you would have come otherwise. You would have thought I had an ulterior motive, when all I want is to cheer you—no, to cheer us both up. Am I right?'

'I suppose you are, yes. Because—well—you're virtually an engaged man. I wouldn't have minded a pub meal—but Valentine's Day—that's only for—couples who are—well, serious. . .' Her voice trailed away. 'I think you know what I'm trying to say.'

'You mean only couples who are in love are here tonight?'

Robyn blushed, and nodded. 'Yes.'

He was quiet for a while. Robyn looked around at the other tables. The pianist played the music from *Casablanca*. He said, 'Maybe there are some couples who are just good friends?' And when she laughed, he said, 'You're beginning to forget all your troubles now?'

'It was a really nice thought. I'm grateful. I suppose February can get a bit grim. There's lots of fun in the year until New Year. Then all of a sudden there's a long stretch of cold dark days.'

'All the colder and darker if you think you're going to lose your job.'

Robyn put her shoulders back and smiled bravely. 'I'm not going to even think it. We're going to win, and Chase Hey is going to go on looking after the Barnaby people from cradle to grave, just as we always have.'

'And you and I in the west wing will go on arguing

and fighting about the best treatment for every patient!
You and your fancy wise woman's ideas, me and my
modern medicine. Do you think we'll go on fighting
until we retire and go into an old folks' home?'

She laughed aloud, and leaned over the table
towards him. 'I shall certainly go on arguing until you
see sense!'

'And I shall go on maintaining that I'm the one who
is talking sense!' In the middle of the laughter he
caught her hands in his. 'Come and dance?'

In his arms, she could almost forget that they were
only good friends, so gently and tenderly did he hold
her. 'This is so very kind of you. I think I'll stop
shouting at you from now on, Paul.'

'No, don't stop. I wouldn't feel comfortable if you
were nice to me.'

'Am I really so awful?'

'I wouldn't say awful—just a pain in the neck.' He
tightened his arms round her for a moment. 'But I
think sometimes I deserve the things you say, and I'm
glad you have the guts to stand up to me when
everyone else licks my boots.'

The candlelit dinner was sheer self-indulgence.
Robyn, who had hardly eaten a decent meal since the
Caribbean feast they'd had on Boxing Day, couldn't
manage half of what was on offer. They chatted as
easily as though they had never quarrelled, and afterwards they danced again, close and warm, until after
midnight. He murmured, 'I hate the thought of leaving, but we both have to be at work tomorrow.'

Robyn said happily, 'I don't mind going. It's been a
great surprise, and I've loved every minute. Thanks,
Paul.' They threaded their way through the other
dancers towards the foyer. The head waiter smiled

indulgently. 'I hope it has been enjoyable, Miss Alexander. Goodnight, madam, sir.'

Robyn sat in the car, her heart turned to ice. She got out before he had time to open the door for her. At the door of the cottage, she turned to Paul. 'It's been a lovely evening, Paul.' Her voice was strained. 'Quite a change from the Three Bells.' Paul held out his hand to take hers, but she made sure it was unavailable. 'I hope I was a suitable stand-in.' And she closed the door in his face.

CHAPTER TWELVE
March

THE West sisters were spending a Saturday morning together. That was unusual in itself, because Mary was getting more and more into the routine of her Amos's smallholding, and they were busy transplanting her herbs and her favourite flowers into their new garden. There was a gleam of sun through the wild clouds, and Mary had brought in some catkins to decorate the dining table.

Robyn said, 'I never thought I'd hear you sing when you're leaving Meadow Cottage.'

'I never thought I'd be so happy. I've known Amos all my life. You remember how he was one of the first to say hello, when we came back from Father's travels, and settled here in our first real home? I've liked Amos all my life. When we worked together in the garden I thought he was just being kind—because of my legs, you know. But all the time he said he wanted to be near me because I made him happy. That's sweet, isn't it, Bobbie?'

'Very sweet,' agreed her sister. Now seemed to be the right time to mention what was on her mind. 'But, now that I'm buying your half of the cottage, you won't mind if I mortgage it, will you?'

Mary turned from the kitchen table, where she was preparing vegetables for a casserole. Her blue eyes were wide. 'You're serious?'

'I am. For the sake of Chase Hey, I am.' She sat up

straight on the chair opposite and looked at Mary with sincerity. 'I know you think it's a daft idea—maybe even criminal of me, I can see it in your eyes—but I can't bear to think of the money not being enough in the action fund. I thought of selling——'

Mary gave a little scream. 'You didn't!'

'Exactly. I knew you'd be furious. Even though people have told me that if we sold we'd be very rich.'

'But you're buying my half from me, so that Amos and I can build up his business. You couldn't buy my share and then let it go to someone awful like Vicki Alexander, could you, Robyn? Not really? Just because she's offering three times the price?'

Robyn shook her head vehemently. 'No, you know I couldn't, and I wouldn't. But mortgaging is different. I borrow the money, then pay it back. The cottage is still mine.' She looked into Mary's face for a reaction. Mary looked bemused. Robyn went on, 'I'd like to get the mortgage arranged before Paul goes to the authority with his details.'

Mary wheeled herself away from the table and round to face her. 'I have to tell you, Bobbie—I've already been asked if I'll sell my half to someone else. Can you imagine? To sell half of Meadow Cottage to someone you may not get on with? It's ludicrous. Naturally, I told the agent I'm not remotely interested.'

Robyn's eyes flashed, and she banged her fist on the arm of the sofa. 'Vicki Alexander has been at you too, has she? Offering about six times as much as I can afford? Is that it? And you weren't even tempted?'

Mary sighed, and wheeled herself towards the kitchen. 'It would be idiotic not to be tempted, Bobbie. You know how badly the market-garden business is doing with all this European competition? Amos is only just breaking even. He'd be glad of money to modernise, and set up some new glass-houses.' She filled the kettle and plugged it in. The sunlight grew stronger, sending golden flashes on the white walls, and the red flagged floor. She turned round again. Robyn was watching her fixedly. 'But I said no. I don't want outsiders in this place any more than you do.'

Robyn jumped up and ran to hug her. 'I knew I could count on you. I'll ring the bank first thing on Monday. No, on second thoughts, I'll do it now. They don't do that sort of business on Saturdays—but I can make sure they know I'll be coming in on Monday, and can start the paperwork!'

'Slow down. They're open till twelve. Let's have a quiet cup of coffee first.' She seemed anxious to restrain her sister, and kept looking at the clock.

'All right. But you know the health authority board is meeting on the seventeenth.'

'Don't panic, Sis. You've time for a cuppa.'

They were just sitting down to their coffee when the doorbell rang. Robyn put her cup down and went to answer it. Paul stood there, in riding breeches and tweed jacket. She had been very distant with her handsome consultant since the night of the Valentine's Dance, but she was suddenly glad to see him, glad she could tell him that she had figured out a way to raise the money the hospital needed. 'Come in, Paul. I've something to tell you!' She took his arm to hurry him up, and put her cup of coffee into his hands.

He seemed pleased that she was friendly again. 'I've something to tell you too. First of all, I've been to

Bragg's. You're not cross with me for going riding without inviting you?'

'Of course not.' She flushed. Paul wasn't her property. They'd hardly been on speaking terms. 'You can go riding with anyone you choose.'

'I went riding with Mr Willy Bragg.'

'With Willy and no one else?'

'Yes. And I asked for Napoleon.' He sipped the coffee. 'You can guess why, maybe?'

'You've always been a bit suspicious about that fall of Mr Black's.'

'Ever since Ross Cartwright told me they'd already had one accident with that horse. Willy was so cagey about showing me Napoleon last time. I knew there was something wrong. He admitted that the horse was temperamental. He also admitted that he knew Black wasn't a very good rider. I bought him a drink or two at the Bells, and it came out that he had a grudge against him for some lawsuit Black lost on his behalf. I inferred that Bragg let him take Napoleon that day without warning him it was the horse that had been in the *Recorder*. Of course, he hasn't admitted it in so many words, but I put two and two together—and netted five thousand pounds! Willy offered it to the fund!' Paul grinned broadly. 'Quite spontaneous, his offer was. He assured me he never allows anyone to ride Napoleon now except himself and his son.'

'That's almost blackmail!'

'The best kind—when a wrong is righted, and the money goes to a good cause.'

Robyn ran her fingers through her hair with a great sigh of relief. 'You've got the money you want, then?'

'All of it. Our documents can be finalised and sent to the health board today!'

'I'm so glad.'

Mary added, 'You don't know how glad! She was just going to raise money on Meadow Cottage. I'm very relieved she doesn't have to. You've no idea how relieved.' She quietly took herself to the kitchen, and pulled the door to, indicating that the other two should take their coffee to the living-room.

Paul said, 'I couldn't let you mortgage your only possession. I wouldn't have accepted it.'

'I wouldn't have told you where it came from.'

Paul leaned back in the chair. Riding clothes suited him, and Robyn was glad that the period of strain was apparently over between them. She had missed their comfortable talks together. Paul said casually, 'I suppose Vicki had offered to buy the place?'

Robyn looked directly at him. 'She won't get it. Mary won't sell to her, and half is mine.'

'I'm glad.' And he smiled at her expression of disbelief. 'I'm very glad. We wouldn't want Vicki Alexander hanging around Barnaby, would we? Ruin the tone of the neighbourhood.'

'What sort of joke is that, Paul? You know as well as I do she was on the cover of *Vogue* last month. I saw the copy in your room. The local snobs would be thrilled to have her as a neighbour.' Robyn realised her voice was rising, and paused to calm herself down. It wasn't ladylike to scream at guests. She said, 'She was quite obviously planning on settling in Barnaby. Why else had she booked that Valentine's dinner that she didn't manage to show up for?'

Paul smiled. 'I'm not responsible for what she was planning, Robyn. I haven't seen her since New Year's Eve.' He looked at his watch. 'I have to go. Shall we ride next Saturday?'

He was changing the subject, but Robyn was happy to leave Vicki's name out of the conversation. New Year's Eve—that was a long time for Vicki to stay away. Could it really be possible that she was losing heart over Paul's fickleness? Robyn said cheerfully enough, 'Will we be in the mood? It's the Saturday before the board's decision. We might be planning a wake.'

'We'll be in the mood. Spring is coming, can't you feel it? Look at the garden, Bobbie. Snowdrops and crocuses under the pear tree. Daffodils pushing through.' He stood at the window, gazing out.

She watched his handsome profile, loving it very dearly. 'I didn't know you bothered much about gardens.'

He turned and picked up his riding crop as he made for the door. 'Just this one, Bobbie—just this garden. It means quite a lot to me.' And he closed the door behind him. Robyn went to the window too, stared out at the new life pushing through the earth that belonged to her. Paul was right. Spring was almost here. She'd been so busy with her plans for the hospital that she had almost forgotten about it. But, now the action fund had the money they needed, there was time to think about real life again. All they had to do was wait until the seventeenth of March.

On the sixteenth, Paul called a quick meeting of the campaign. 'The health authority have all my documents. It's in their hands now. They've asked me to attend the meeting at eleven in the morning, so I should be back by one to tell you what they decided.'

Tom Gordon stood up, and walked round the table towards Paul. He held out his hand. 'This is it, then. At the beginning, Paul, I have to admit I didn't think we had a chance. But you've done a magnificent job. Thanks. I have to say I think it's better than fifty-fifty now. We all know the board has to save money. But we've raised our own. And, if anyone could show them what a dynamic team we have here, I say it's Paul Howell-Jones, our lucky Welshman!'

Paul gripped his hand. 'I'm the one who should say thank you. Your important word was "team", Tom. I can't thank you all enough for the sheer blood and guts you've put into this.' His voice was suddenly hoarse, and he cleared his throat as Tom shook his hand hard.

Robyn was returning to the ward when she heard running footsteps, and a breathless Paul caught up with her. There was a suspicious brightness in his eyes. She knew he had a tender emotional side, but he had never let it show before. She stopped while he caught his breath. They stood together in the deserted corridor. She liked the way he didn't try to hide his feelings. When he didn't speak, she said quietly, 'We've had a good time, Paul, with your action committee. Learnt a lot and given a lot too. Even if we—have to split up and go to different quarters of the compass, we won't forget this year.'

He looked into her eyes. 'But I still hate losing. It's something to do with my early life, I think—my dad so easily gave up and thought success wasn't for the likes of us. . . I had to prove that success isn't everything, but that shouldn't stop anyone from having a damn good shot. The likes of us can win just the same as anyone else.' He looked down at her as they both leaned against the window-sill in a natural way, like old friends. 'You know, Bobbie, you're the only one in this town I've told about my family? Shows what a superficial bastard I am, doesn't it?'

She felt her maternal affection coming on. 'Maybe we've all done things from sentiment—from heart rather than head. Doesn't that just about put us in the human race?'

His green eyes were openly affectionate as he looked into hers. 'More than anything, I'd be sorry if I lost touch with you. Will that happen, do you think?'

Didn't he realise that neither of them could decide that? It was up to Victoria Alexander, and Robyn knew very well what her ambitions were, in spite of her not seeing Paul since January. To be the centre of Paul Howell-Jones's life. Robyn smiled up at him, sadly. Buying even the whole of Meadow Cottage couldn't achieve that. Sending Vicki to Outer Mongolia couldn't achieve that. The only way to be sure of him forever would be to share his caring of his patients, and to agree on how to do it. If only he could open his mind just a little bit more. . .

Robyn sighed suddenly, and tried to suppress the sigh. She said firmly, 'Now you know you're not going to lose. Not now. Not ever. Your Welsh ancestors are seeing to that!'

They resumed their walk towards the ward. Somehow his arm found her shoulders as they walked, and Robyn didn't think it was wrong to be so close while at work, and didn't try to shake it off. He said, 'What did you call it, Bobbie? Not black magic but tender magic?' He shook his head suddenly, and dropped his arm.

Robyn decided that he was thinking of his beautiful Vicki. It was a pity that young lady hadn't been around more. Then Robyn wouldn't have been his companion

on so many gallops, so many dinners, so many eve-
nings in the Three Bells. It would be hard to see him
with Vicki, when they had been such friends. Such
very good friends. Even though she was only a stand-
in.

They were coming to the ward doors. She had to
face her loneliness with fortitude. She did it by saying,
'I bet it's you who starts the first fight!'

And he laughed, and tried to smack her on the
bottom, but she ran too fast, and was inside before he
got there, the door swinging back into his face.

He did his ward-round meticulously, before the meeting with the board. He even saw some out-patients,
before handing over to his registrar. Robyn said
nothing apart from work, knowing that he felt as she
did—that all the talking had been done, and all they
really had to do now was wait.

The members of the campaign committee began
drifting towards Paul's consulting-rooms at about a
quarter to one. They draped themselves on the desk,
on the examination couch, against the window and in
the chairs. They said very little. One o'clock came and
went. Half-past one came and went, and John
Crabtree proclaimed his blood sugar to be low, and
sent a domestic to bring them a pot of tea and some
ham rolls.

There was a hesitant tap on the door, and the pale
determined face of Philomena Gorsey peeped round.
She searched the room until she saw Robyn. 'Sister,
can I tell you something?'

Robyn wasn't in the mood for talking just now, but
she couldn't send Phil away, little Philomena, who had
trusted Robyn—and Chase Hey—throughout her

uncertain and troubled life. She went to the door and out into the corridor. There she opened her eyes in surprise, to see Kevin holding Phil's hand. He cleared his throat, and with a glance at Phil, confessed, 'We— that is, she—thought we ought to do something, miss. I mean Sister. So we wrote to the health people, and told them how good you've been to our Phil. I hope we didn't do wrong, miss. She said it were right to tell them how many times you've looked after her when nobody else cared.'

Robyn could do nothing else but hug the girl to her, not trying to hide the tears in her eyes. 'It's the best thing anyone could ever have done,' she managed to say as she wished them well, and made sure she had their new address so that she could call and see the baby when it was born. 'Even if the news here is bad, I'll remember today as a happy day, Phil. Thanks, love.'

At a quarter to two a junior nurse tapped on the door. 'Dr Howell-Jones says would you meet him in the canteen, sir?' And the assembled committee made a dignified but hurried charge along to the canteen. There were many more staff in the canteen, all waiting for Paul, all very well aware where he had been. He turned from the counter, where he had returned his coffee-cup. His face was a blank, as he paused to make sure everyone was in and the doors closed. Then he said simply but clearly, 'We've done it.'

There was a spontaneous outburst of cheers and whistles. Staff made for telephones, for all the world like the Press corps at the White House after the President had made some momentous statement. 'We've done it. We've done it. We've done it.' The

kitchen staff broke into a jubilant conga, and Paul
Howell-Jones began to smile.

There was a raised dais at one end of the room,
where musicians played when they hád a staff party.
Paul was lifted shoulder-high and carried to the stage,
and a speech was demanded. He raised his hands to
calm the shouting, but for a while it was impossible to
quell the genuine appreciation his colleagues wanted
to show him. After several minutes, silence fell.

'Ladies and gentlemen, we've done it. What more
do you want me to say?'

He received suggestions, some polite, some frivo-
lous. John Crabtree said, 'What swung it, Paul? Did
they say?'

'Well, they were impressed, naturally, by our ability
to raise the money and invest it wisely. I believe they
are coming to take lessons from our campaign committee, so that they can let the government know how
it can be done!' There were more cheers then, and
whistles from the more exuberant housemen.

Paul raised his hands again. 'Mr Swainson Black
told me himself that he had nothing but praise for our
set-up here. He told everyone of his own good treatment here, and he read out a letter of apprecation he'd
had from a young patient who reckoned she wouldn't
have made it but for us, which brought a lump to his
throat, he said. He did hand me a personal letter, too,
but I don't think now is the time to read it.'

'Read it! Read it!' The letter was found in his
pocket, and read for him.

I was soon to find out from my own unfortunate
accident that Chase Hey don't just put a man
together again as a body, they care about him as a

person. It took a long time, and I was a difficult case, but you, Dr Howell-Jones, never gave up on me, and I don't forget that kind of care in a hurry. I was also impressed by your willingness to consider alternative treatments at my suggestion. Your arcade, put together originally as a financial set-up, has turned into an asset for your patients, in that they can find many branches of healing under one roof. This is a bold and imaginative project, very much to be praised, and, one hopes, copied by other hospitals in the area. In my opinion, Chase Hey combines state and private treatment in a harmonious and successful way, and I intend to promote some of these ideas when I undertake a lecture tour later in the year.

By this time the room was full, and patients in dressing-gowns could be seen filling the corridors outside. Paul stood up again and acknowledged the cheering. He said, when he could make himself heard, 'I'd like to acknowledge something to you all now. You're not cheering Howell-Jones today. It was a joint effort and if I'd not listened to colleagues I wouldn't be in this happy place now. I want you all to give my ward sister the cheers you've given me, because, without the many and severe tellings-off from Robyn West, I'd still never have taken the trouble to investigate the alternative side of our profession. I'd still be in the Dark Ages. Thanks, Robyn.' He held out his hand to her as she was projected up on the platform beside him. He gave her a kiss on the cheek, which received more cheers, then he said simply, 'Robyn, thank you. You more than anyone should share in this triumph. No one knows what you were willing to give to save this hospital. We've shared a lot this year. Will you share the rest of your life with me too? And make it as happy as this year has been?'

In the tumult Robyn didn't realise what he had said, and wondered why the cheering was getting louder, and why Paul was taking her in his arms. 'You pretended all along that you were still against my ideas,' she protested in his ear.

'Yes. It was fun, wasn't it, fighting with me?'

'I suppose it was.' She was too elated to maintain her protest. 'Yes, of course it was. We'll have to think of something else to fight about now.' The others were still shouting, and she turned to Paul to ask why.

'You haven't answered my proposal,' he grinned.

'Proposal?'

'I asked you to give me the rest of your life.'

'In front of——? Did you mean it?'

His look told her. The rest of the room disappeared for a moment, as Paul took her closely into his arms, and held her extremely tightly, knocking her cap off, and causing her hair to lose its restraining pins and to fall loose around her flushed and happy face.

Much later they sat together in the dark room of Meadow Cottage, lit only by the low flickering fire. Outside, although dusk had fallen, the thrushes and blackbirds still trilled of their love in ecstatic chorus. Robyn sat curled up on the carpet, her arms on Paul's knees. They were both silent now, exhausted by the day's excitement, and the enormity of the first ecstatic fulfilment of their own love.

'Are you hungry?' whispered Robyn, too happy herself to care whether she ate or not.

'A bit. Want to go out?'

'No. I'll fix you something here. I wonder what's

happened to Mary? I thought she would be dying to find out——'

'Er—I rang her. Well, she did ask me to let her know. She's staying with Amos and his mother tonight. She congratulated us—about the hospital.'

Robyn was smiling. 'Oh, Paul, I'm not blind. She knew very well you were going to get the money from Willy Bragg, that Saturday when she wouldn't let me go and mortgage the cottage. You and Mary have seen each other a lot more than I suspected.'

His hand, already enmeshed in her hair, and stirring passions that she thought had been assuaged, swirled it into a tangle as he pulled her into a closer embrace. 'Confession time, my sweetheart. I told Mary I wanted to marry you—but only because she asked me if I was off duty on the date of their marriage. Typical of Mary. She wanted to make sure I came too.'

'What did you say?'

Paul turned her face up to look at him, and kissed her before admitting, 'I asked if it could be a double wedding.'

Robyn sat up. 'You thought I'd accept you? I can't think why!'

Paul looked contrite. 'Call it intuition?'

Robyn shook her head in playful exasperation. 'Don't you know how studiously I had been telling myself that Victoria had a commitment with you? She told me so. You were buying a house together—in Dulwich.'

'May I correct her description of the contract? She—Vicki—was looking for a house I'd like. She kept finding one and I kept refusing. She had never been turned down before. So she was quite cross—took you in too over the cottage. I'm sorry, love. I told her on New Year's Eve that I loved you.'

Exulting in her unexpected triumph, in her total joy, Robyn said, 'Are there any other mistakes I've made, darling? Any secrets I don't know? I'd like to know in advance from now on if anyone has tried to make a fool out of me.'

'Well——'

'There are? I can't believe it! I ought to make you pay for this!'

'It's only that I asked Mary if I could buy her half of Meadow Cottage. Well—you wouldn't want me to stay here as a lodger, would you?'

'It was you! I thought it was Vicki. Well, what price have you offered?'

He pretended to be offended. 'My dear, that is surely a secret between vendor and purchaser!'

Robyn put her hand up to his cheek, and her voice was soft. 'You've paid them more than I could because you know Amos could do with a little extra. You don't have to spell it out. I think I know you, my dear. And I think—because of all the good things I know—that I can forgive old Owen Glendower a lot. Your temper has made me cry—but so has your kindness, love. I'm a lucky woman.' After a long exploratory kiss, during which Paul changed his mind about letting her go to the kitchen to cook for him, Robyn said, 'I suppose I won't be able to be Mary's bridesmaid, if we're both brides?'

'Are you sorry?'

'What do you think? I've never been a bridesmaid before. Now I never will be.'

'I can see how very upsetting that must be, sweetheart.'

She smiled up at him in the firelight. 'I don't think anything will ever upset me again. Are husbands allowed to work in the same ward as their wives?'

He shook his head. 'It's hospital policy not to allow it. But I'll make sure we're not too far away!'

She said sleepily, 'As you're the man who saved the hospital single-handed, I'm sure the management will be on your side.'

'I didn't do anything single-handed. It took a whole lot of work from a whole lot of wonderful people, and the essential ingredient—do you know what the essential ingredient was?'

'Tell me, love?' She reached up her arm to pull him even closer.

'Something you taught me, something that put the heart into all we did, Bobbie.' He paused, and bent to kiss her closed eyelids. 'Your tender magic. . .'

From the author of Mirrors comes an enchanting romance

PATRICIA MATTHEWS

Caught in the steamy heat of America's New South, Rebecca Trenton finds herself torn between two brothers – she yearns for one, but a dark secret binds her to the other.

Off the coast of South Carolina lay Pirate's Bank – a small island as intriguing as the legendary family that lived there. As the mystery surrounding the island deepened, so Rebecca was drawn further into the family's dark secret – and only one man's love could save her from the treachery which now threatened her life.

W🌑RLDWIDE

Mills & Boon

Discover the thrill of 4 Exciting Medical Romances – FREE

FREE

BOOKS FOR YOU

In the exciting world of modern medicine, the emotions of true love have an added drama. Now you can experience four of these unforgettable romantic tales of passion and heartbreak FREE – and look forward to a regular supply of Mills & Boon Medical Romances delivered direct to your door!

❧ ❧ ❧

Turn the page for details of 2 extra free gifts, and how to apply.

An Irresistible Offer from Mills & Boon

Here's an offer from Mills & Boon to become a regular reader of Medical Romances. To welcome you, we'd like you to have four books, a cuddly teddy and a special MYSTERY GIFT, all absolutely free and without obligation.

Then, every month you could look forward to receiving 4 more **brand new** Medical Romances for £1.60 each, delivered direct to your door, post and packing free. Plus our newsletter featuring author news, competitions, special offers, and lots more.

This invitation comes with no strings attached. You can cancel or suspend your subscription at any time, and still keep your free books and gifts.

Its so easy. Send no money now. Simply fill in the coupon below and post it at once to -

Mills & Boon Reader Service, FREEPOST,
PO Box 236, Croydon, Surrey CR9 9EL

NO STAMP REQUIRED

- - - - - ✂ -

YES! Please rush me my 4 Free Medical Romances and 2 Free Gifts! Please also reserve me a Reader Service Subscription. If I decide to subscribe, I can look forward to receiving 4 brand new Medical Romances every month for just £6.40, delivered direct to my door. Post and packing is free, and there's a free Mills & Boon Newsletter. If I choose not to subscribe I shall write to you within 10 days - I can keep the books and gifts whatever I decide. I can cancel or suspend my subscription at any time. I am over 18.

EP20D

Name (Mr/Mrs/Ms) ———————————————

Address ————————————————————

————————————————————————

————————————————— Postcode —————

Signature————————————————————